123 SESAME STREET

happy healthy monsters

WHAT'S OUR FIRST MOVE?
YOUR TURN March in place!
This is a simple uppy-downy movement called jumping!
YOUR TURN Jump!
BOING!

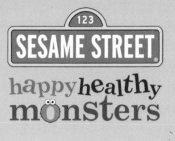

MAKING THE MOST OF JR. CINE-MANGA®

Books use lots of creative techniques to tell stories. The speech balloons and sound effects in comic-style stories are an exciting way for your child to experience the printed word. Here's how you can make the experience even more interactive and playful:

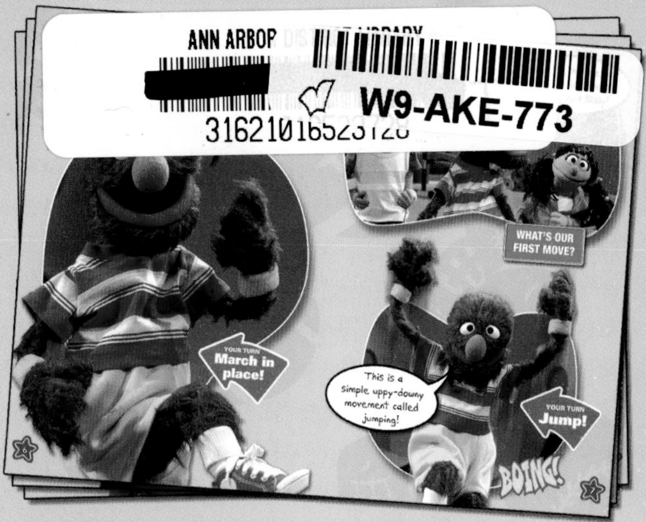

- The first pages introduce the characters and the story. Point to the portraits as you name Grover and his friends. When you revisit the book, ask your child to tell you who everyone is as you point to their labels and ask what they think the story will be about.

- As you read aloud, point to the words in the speech balloons and other words on the page. As you return to the stories, you'll find that kids will "read" some of the words along with you, especially the sound effects. Pages should be read from top to bottom, first the left-hand page, then the right.

- Change your voice from character to character. You don't have to match Grover's funny tones exactly...kids will get a kick out of any goofy voices you put on.

- Cine-Manga uses dynamic photos. Whenever you see an arrow that says "Your Turn," encourage your child to mimic the actions they see the characters performing: jump, pretend to bounce a ball, name your favorite healthy food.

The look of comic books may be different from other picture books, but your child can learn and grow with them the same way they do with other stories. Visual storytelling can motivate children to communicate with pictures and the written word—the best of both worlds!

Senior Editor - Elizabeth Hurchalla
Graphic Designer and Letterer - John Lo
Cover Designers - Anne Marie Horne, Anna Kernbaum and Tomás Montalvo-Lagos

Digital Imaging Manager - Chris Buford
Production Managers - Jennifer Miller and Mutsumi Miyazaki
Senior Designer - Anna Kernbaum
Art Director - Matt Alford
Managing Editor - Jill Freshney
VP of Production - Ron Klamert
Editor in Chief - Mike Kiley
President & C.O.O. - John Parker
Publisher & C.E.O. - Stuart Levy

Written by CHRISTINE FERRARO
Photographs by RICHARD TERMINE
Starring The Muppets™ of Sesame Street
ERIC JACOBSON
KEVIN CLASH
FRAN BRILL
DAVID RUDMAN

E-mail: info@TOKYOPOP.com
Come visit us online at www.TOKYOPOP.com

A **TOKYOPOP** Cine-Manga® Book
TOKYOPOP Inc.
5900 Wilshire Blvd., Suite 2000
Los Angeles, CA 90036

sesameworkshop™
The nonprofit educational organization
behind Sesame Street and so much more
www.sesameworkshop.org

Sesame Street: Happy, Healthy, Monsters

ISBN: 1-59532-826-2

First TOKYOPOP® printing: July 2005

10 9 8 7 6 5 4 3 2 1

Printed in the USA

SESAME STREET
123

happy healthy monsters

TOKYOPOP®

HAMBURG · LONDON · LOS ANGELES · TOKYO

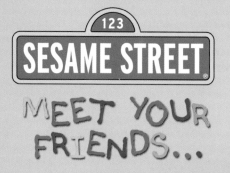

SESAME STREET

MEET YOUR FRIENDS...

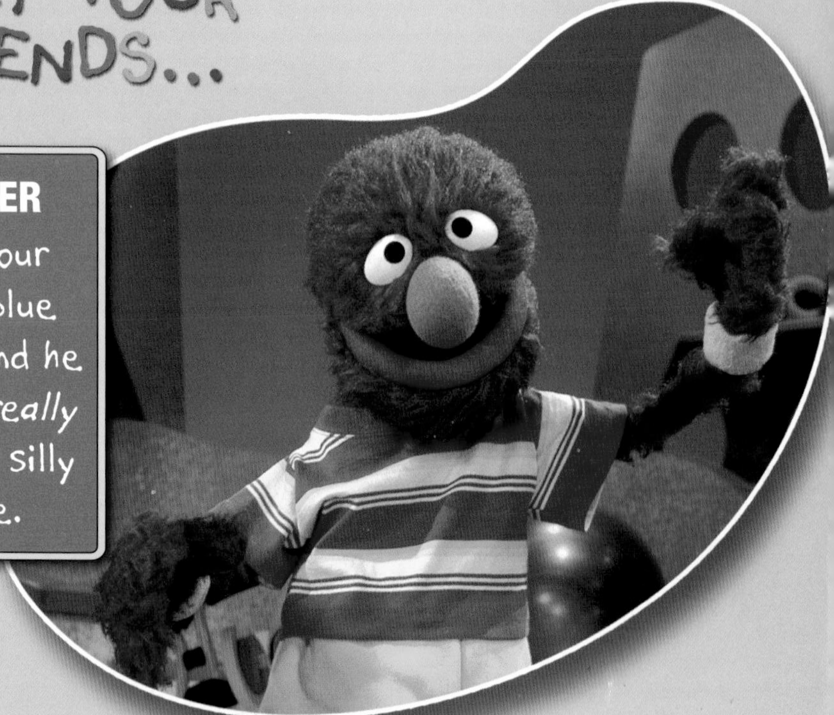

GROVER

He's your furry blue friend and he really, *really* likes to silly dance.

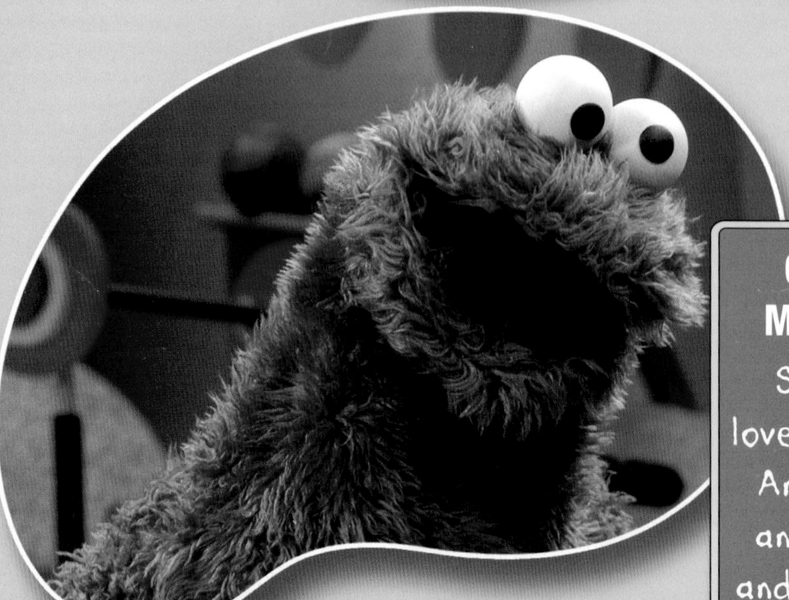

COOKIE MONSTER

Sure, he loves cookies. And milk... and fruit... and cheese...

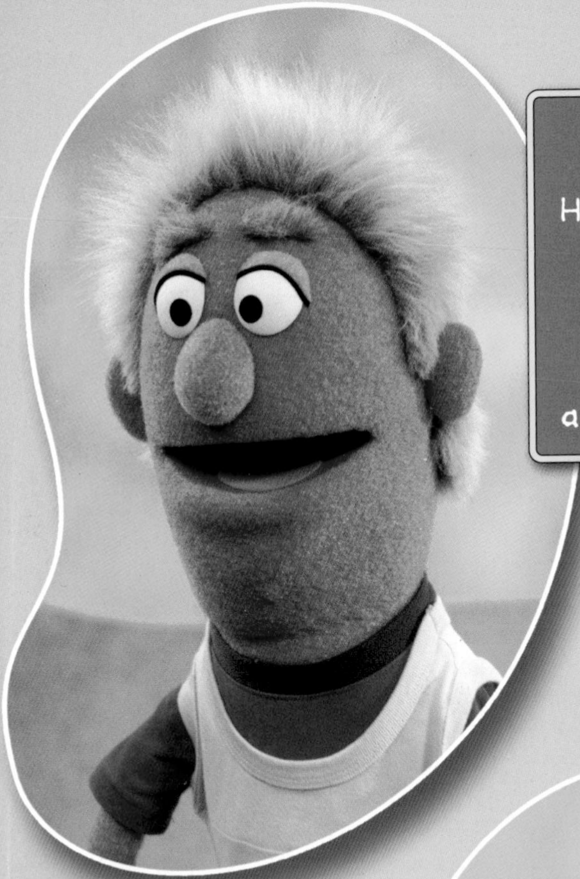

BOBBY

He helps Grover get moving. Bobby thinks jumping jacks are "awesome."

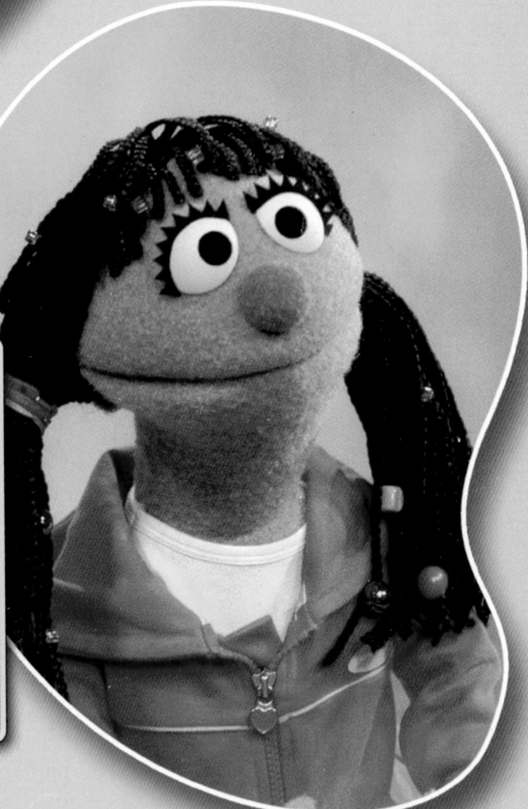

SISSY

Sissy likes stretching best. She's got strong muscles and a great big heart.

GROVER STARTS THE DAY WITH A WARM-UP STRETCH. THEN IT'S TIME TO GET MOVING!

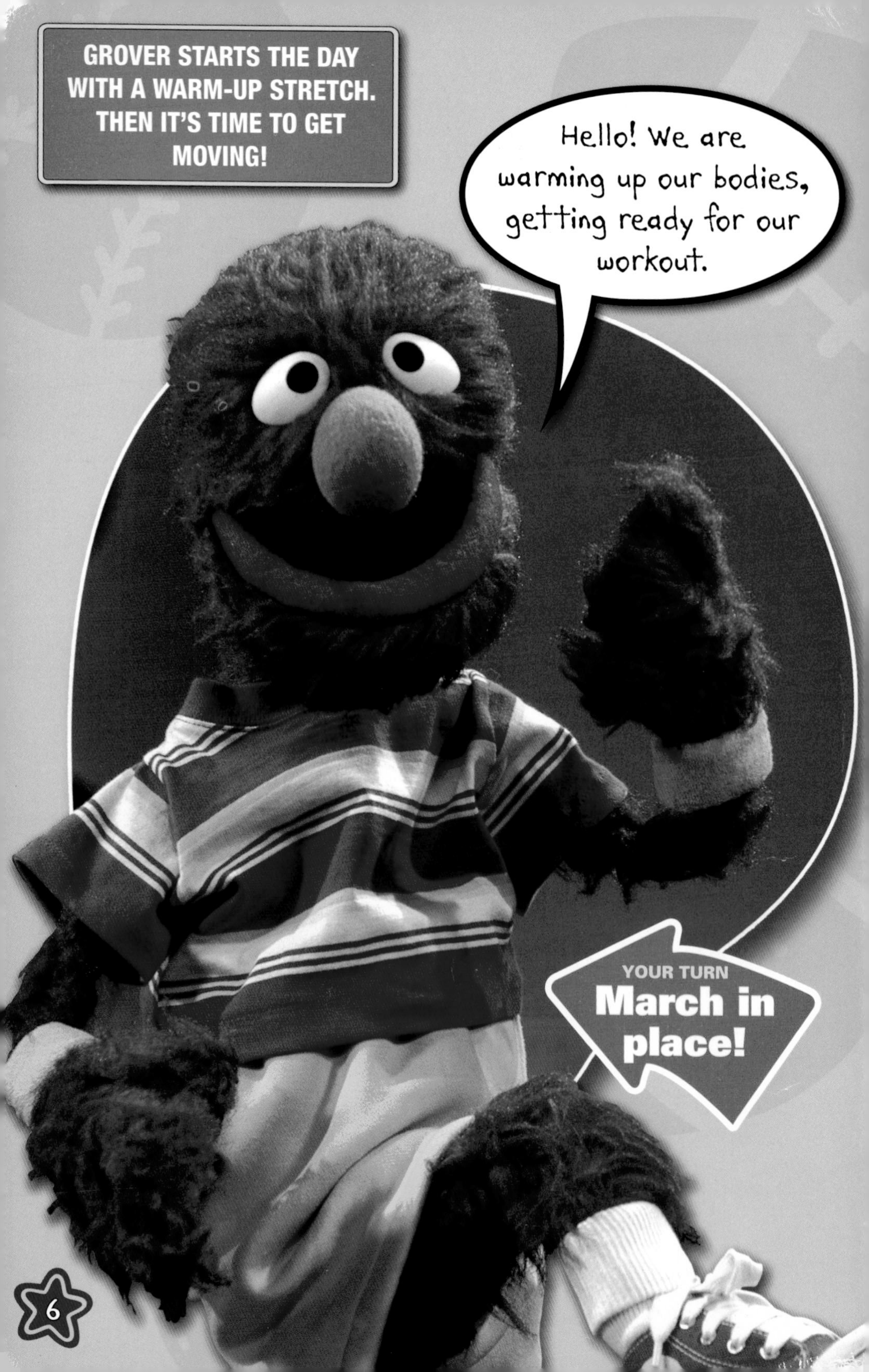
Hello! We are warming up our bodies, getting ready for our workout.
YOUR TURN
March in place!

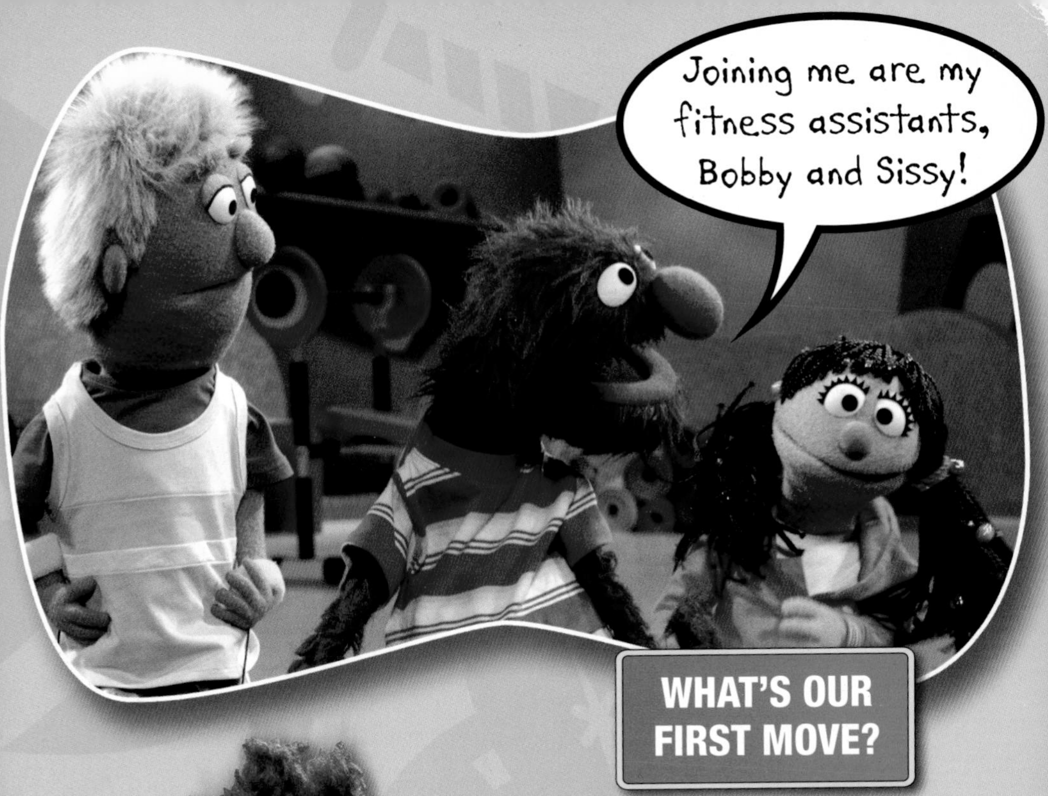

Joining me are my fitness assistants, Bobby and Sissy!
WHAT'S OUR FIRST MOVE?

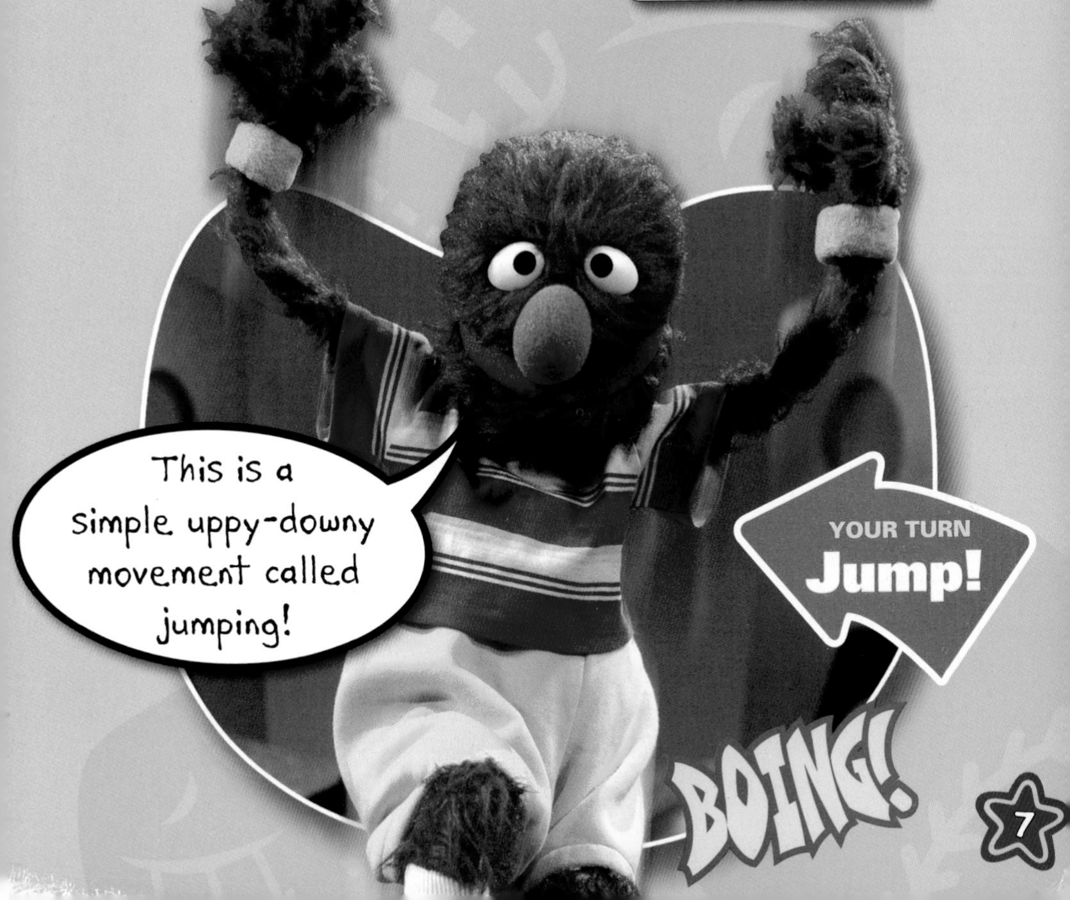

This is a simple uppy-downy movement called jumping!
YOUR TURN Jump!
BOING!

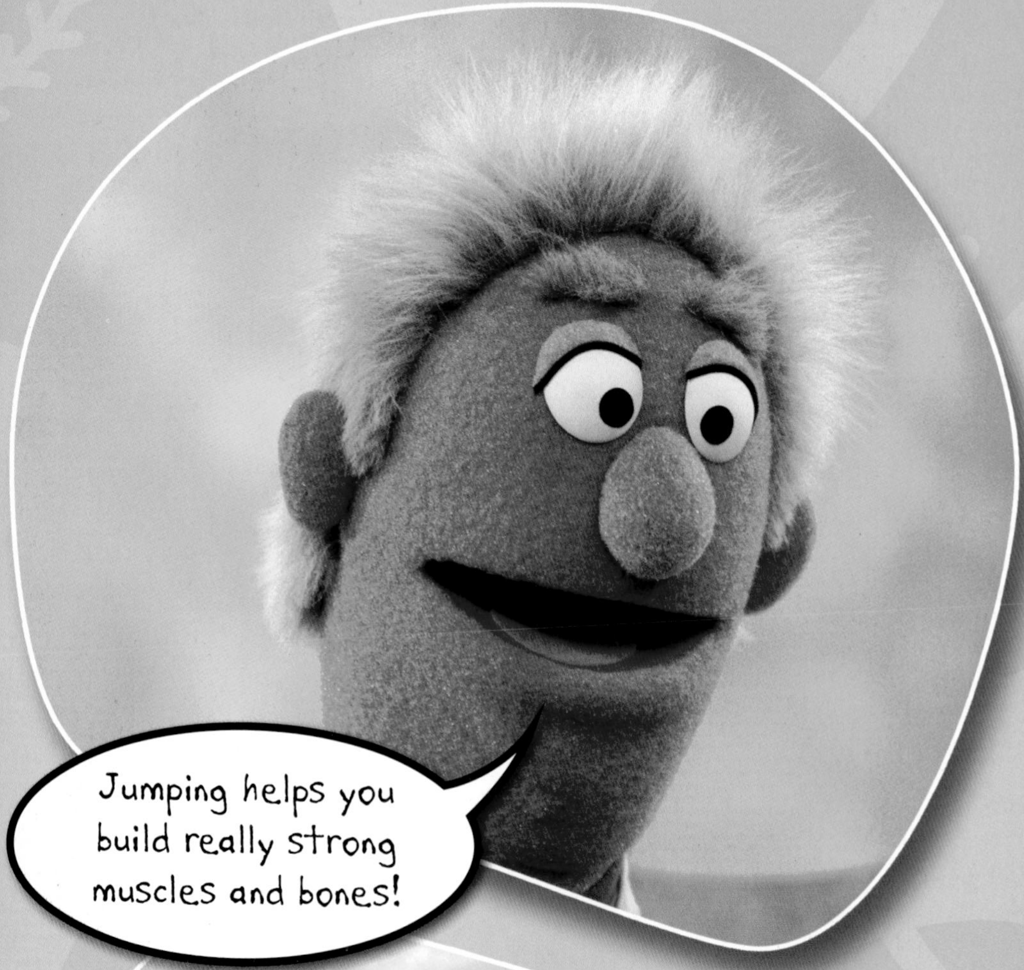
Jumping helps you build really strong muscles and bones!

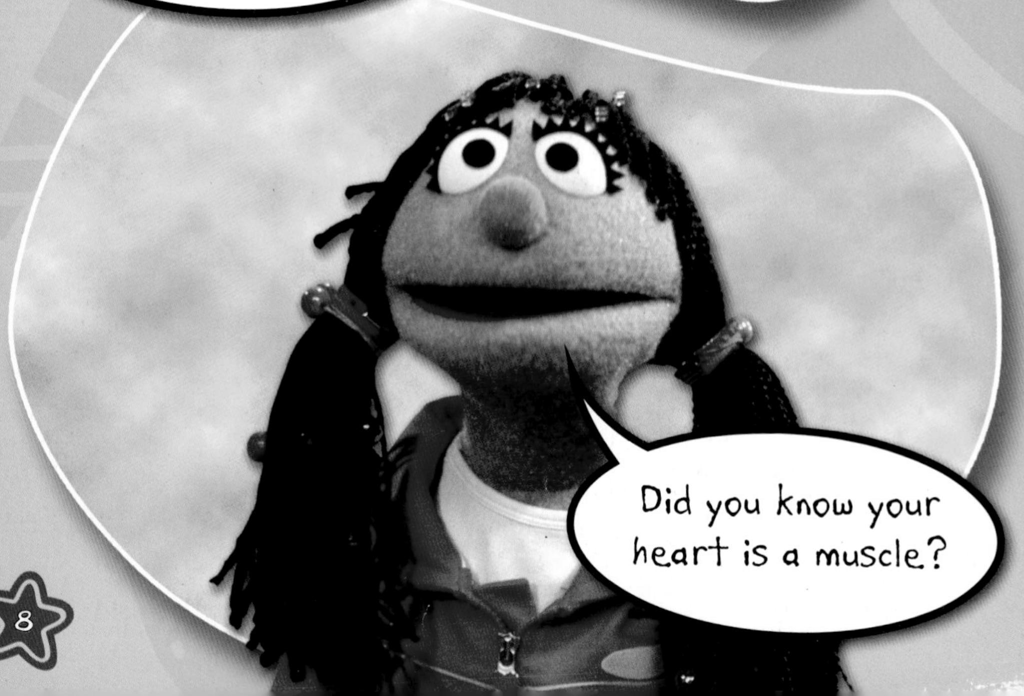
Did you know your heart is a muscle?

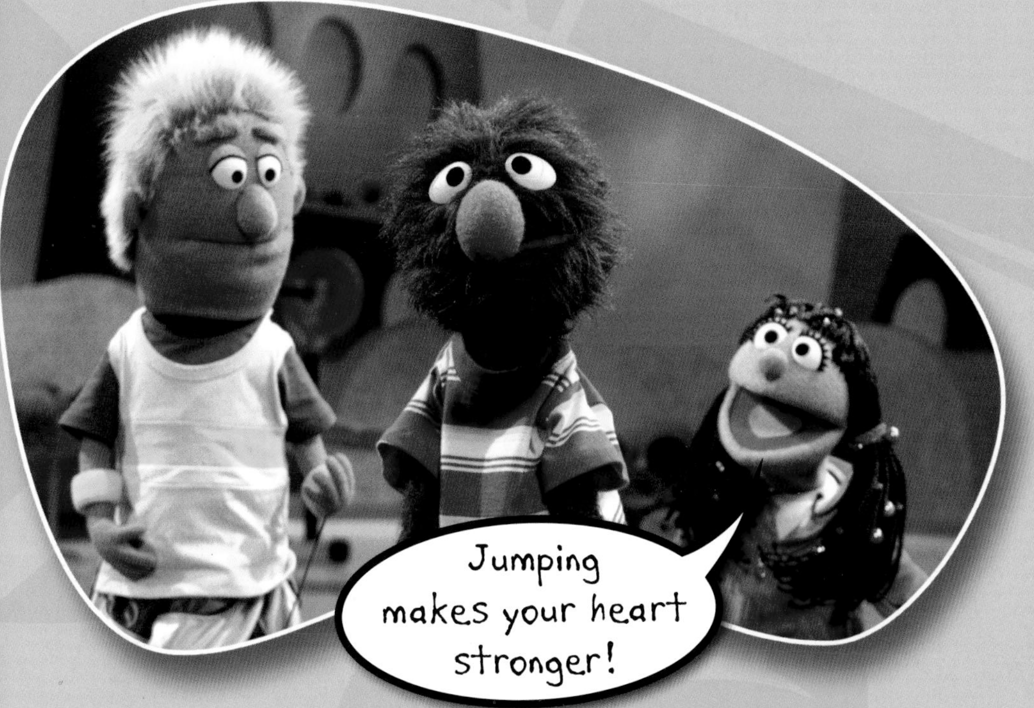
Jumping makes your heart stronger!

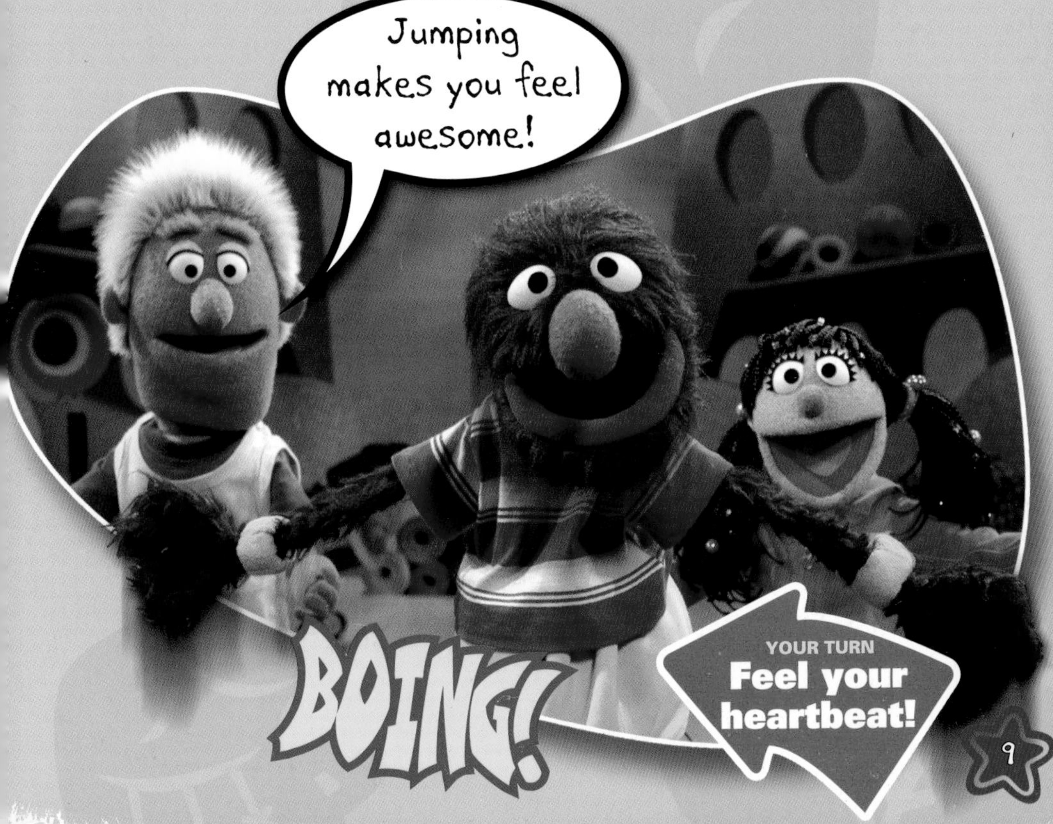
Jumping makes you feel awesome!
BOING!
YOUR TURN
Feel your heartbeat!

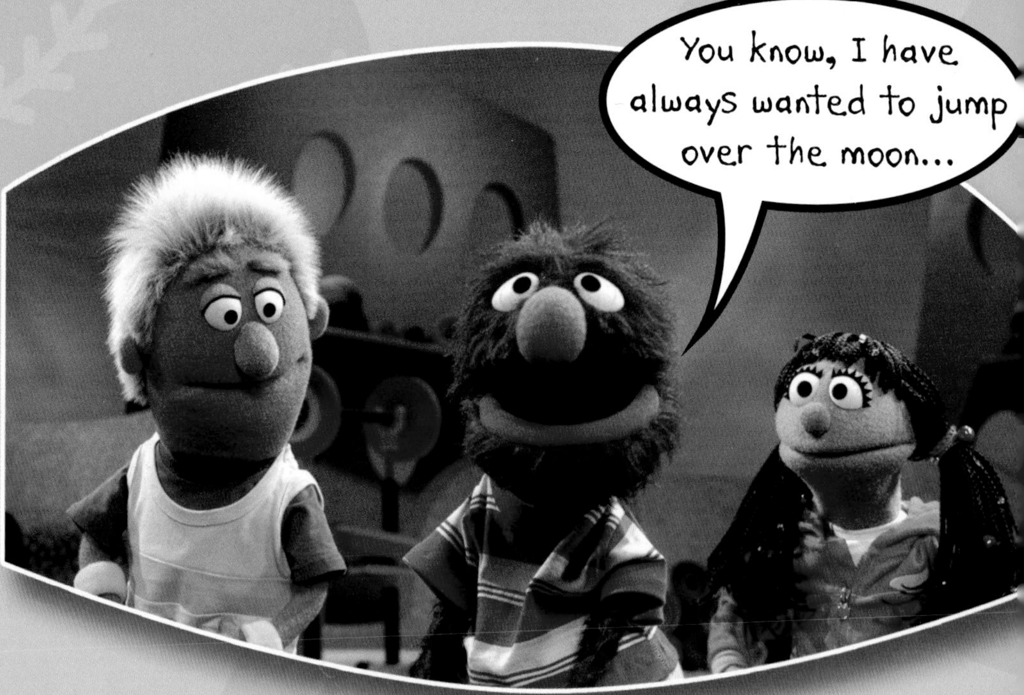
You know, I have always wanted to jump over the moon...

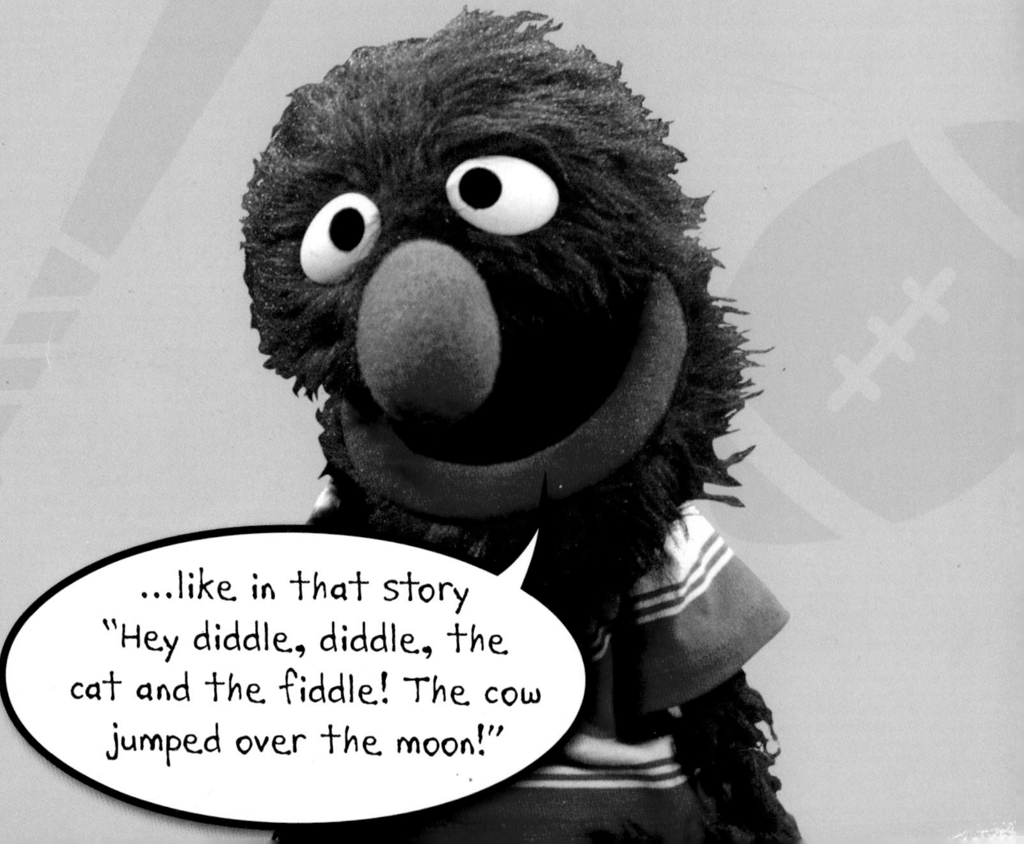
...like in that story "Hey diddle, diddle, the cat and the fiddle! The cow jumped over the moon!"

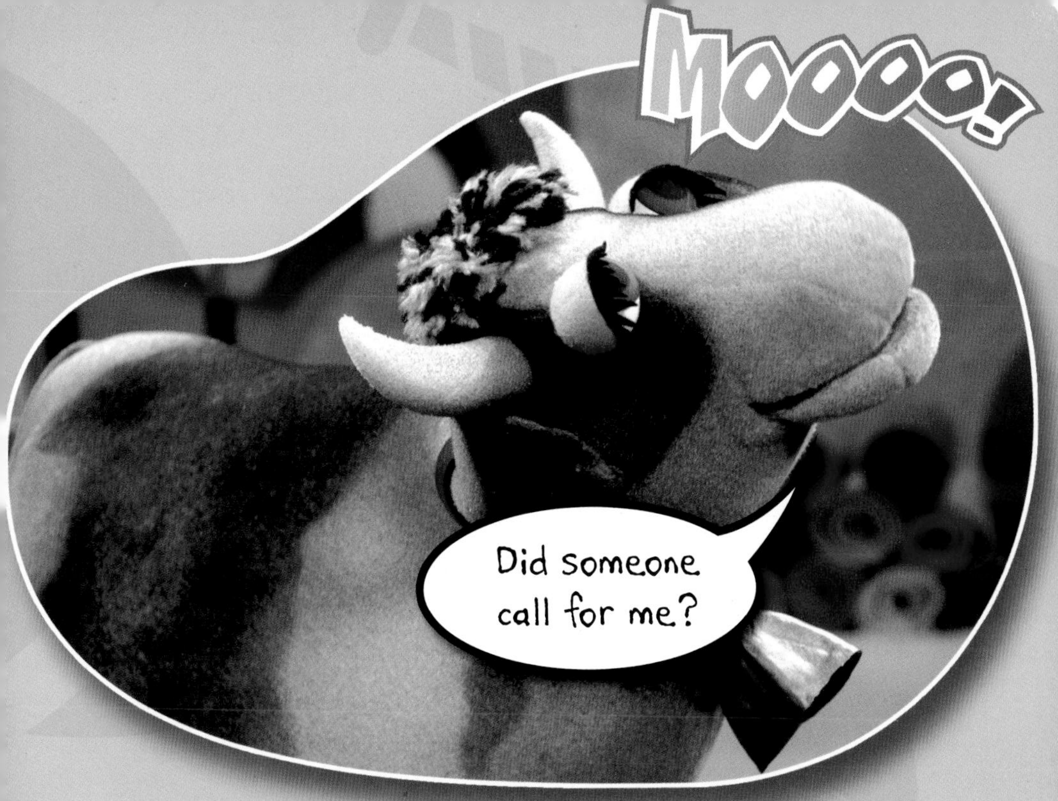
MOOOO!
Did someone call for me?

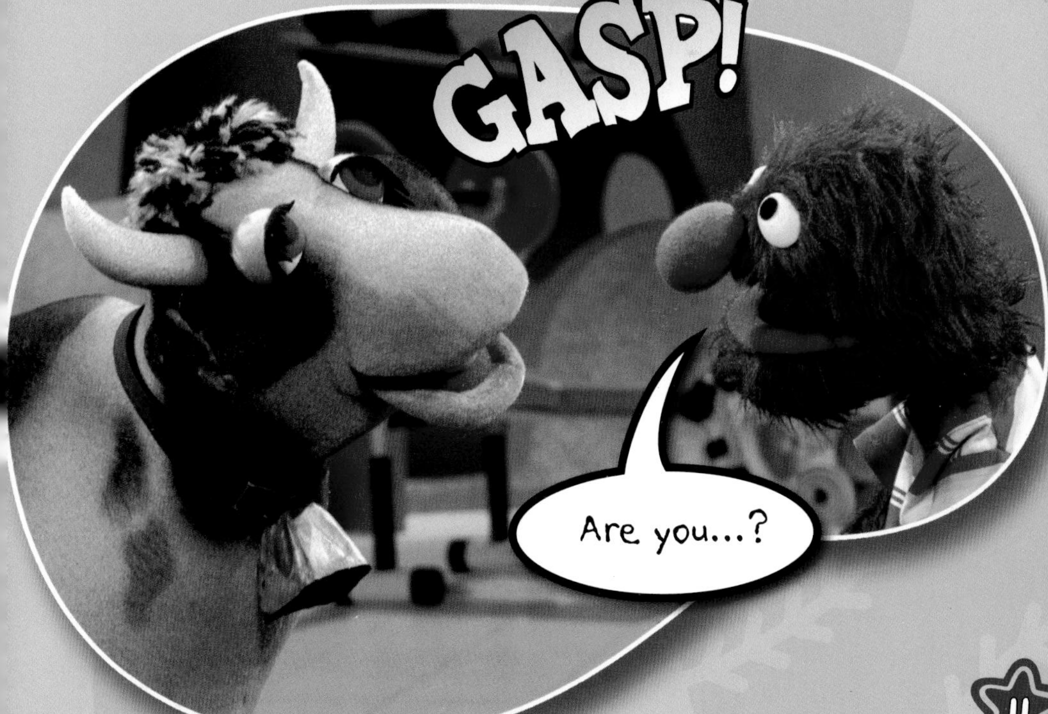
GASP!
Are you...?

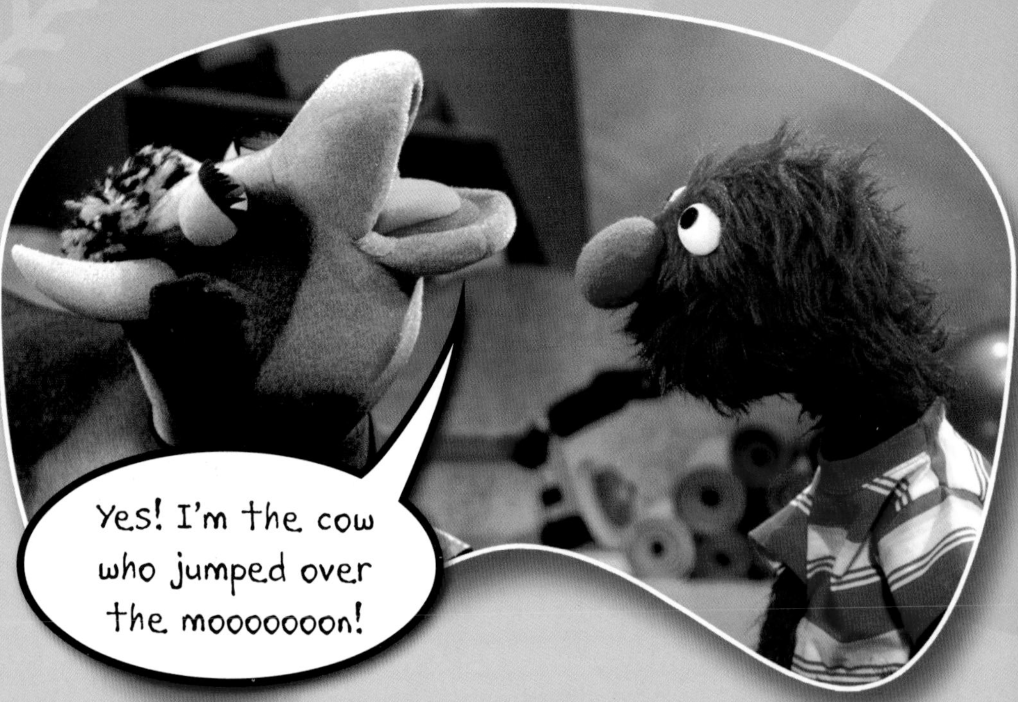
Yes! I'm the cow who jumped over the mooooooon!

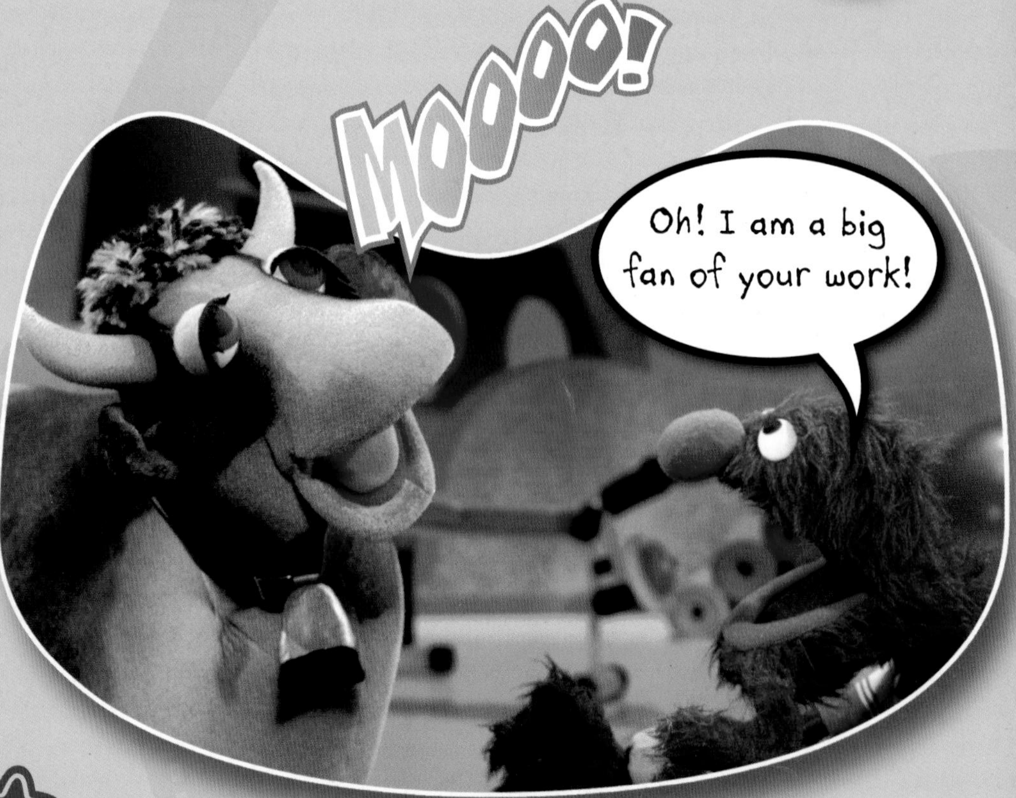
MOOOO!
Oh! I am a big fan of your work!

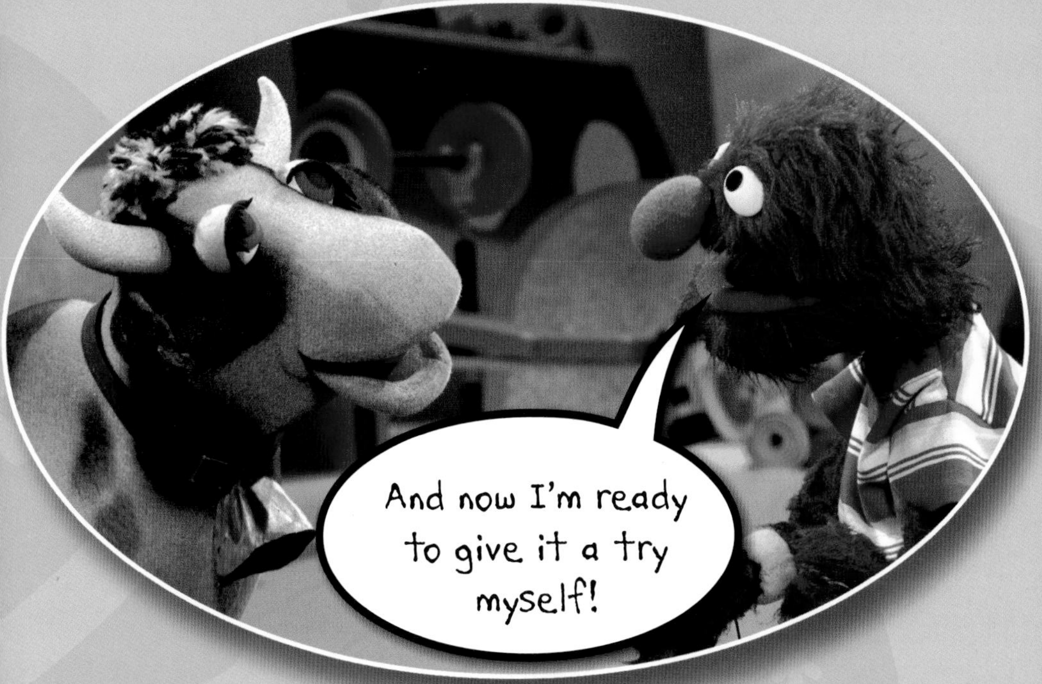
And now I'm ready to give it a try myself!

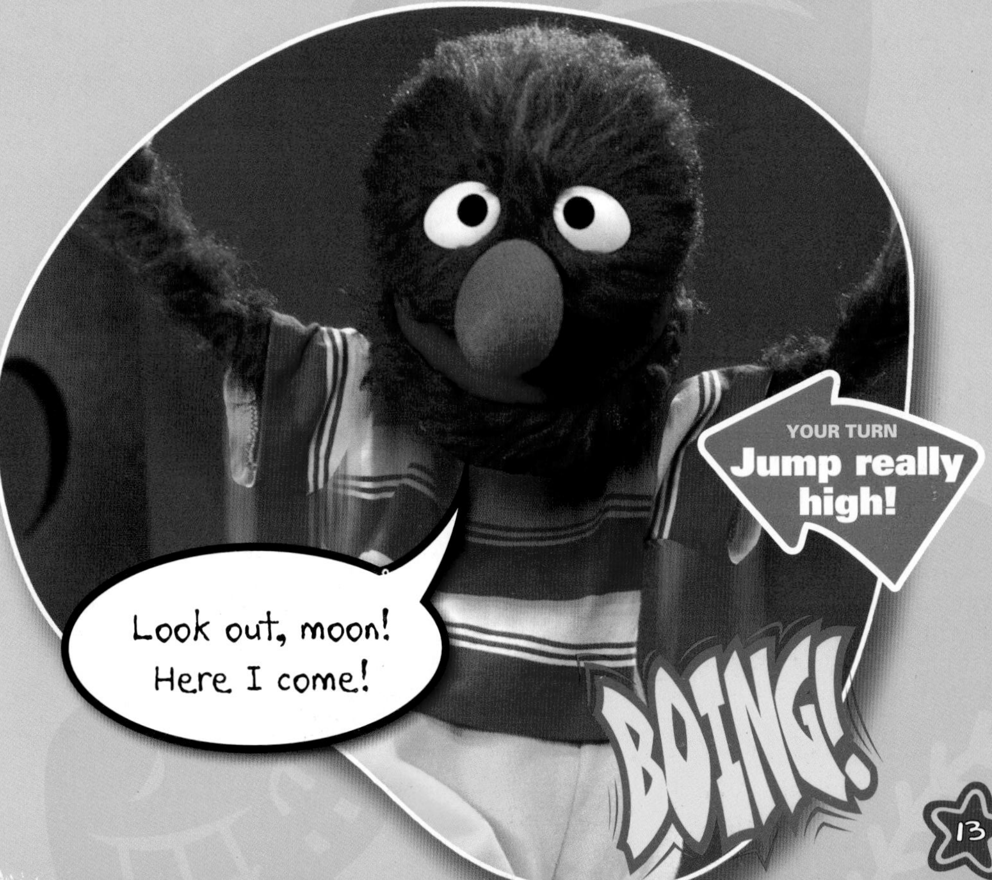
YOUR TURN
Jump really high!
Look out, moon! Here I come!
BOING!

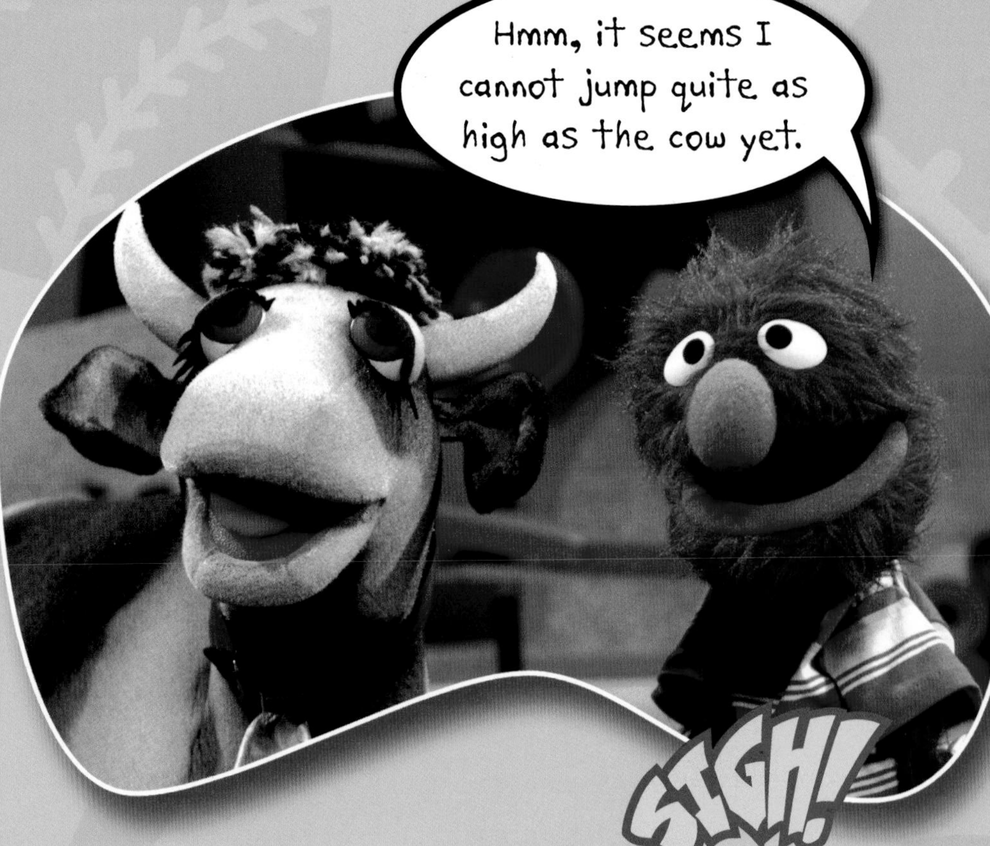
Hmm, it seems I cannot jump quite as high as the cow yet.
SIGH!

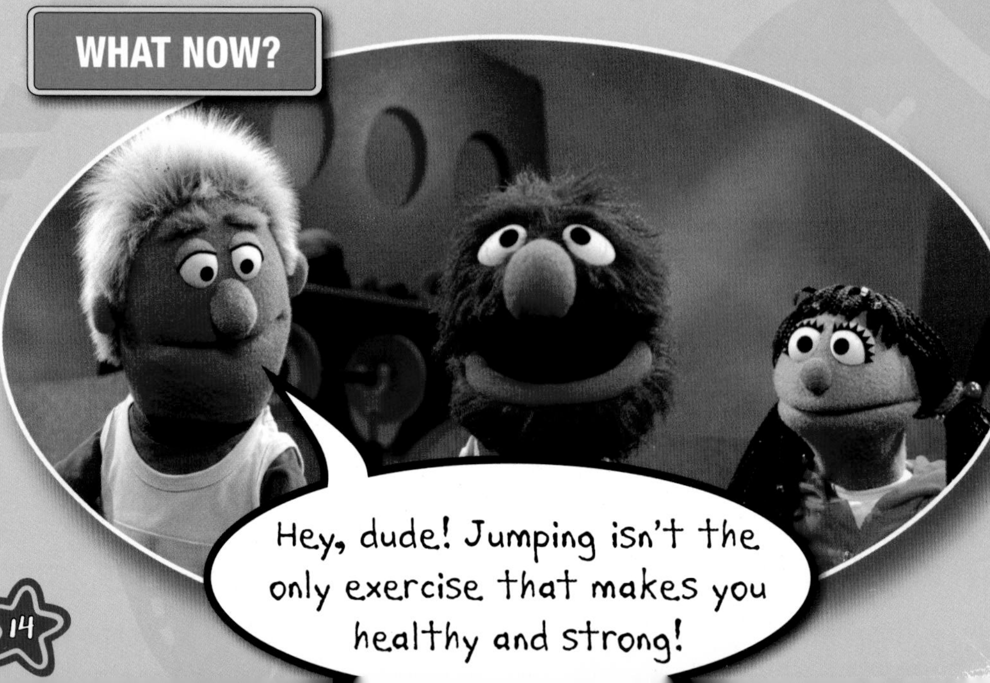
WHAT NOW?
Hey, dude! Jumping isn't the only exercise that makes you healthy and strong!

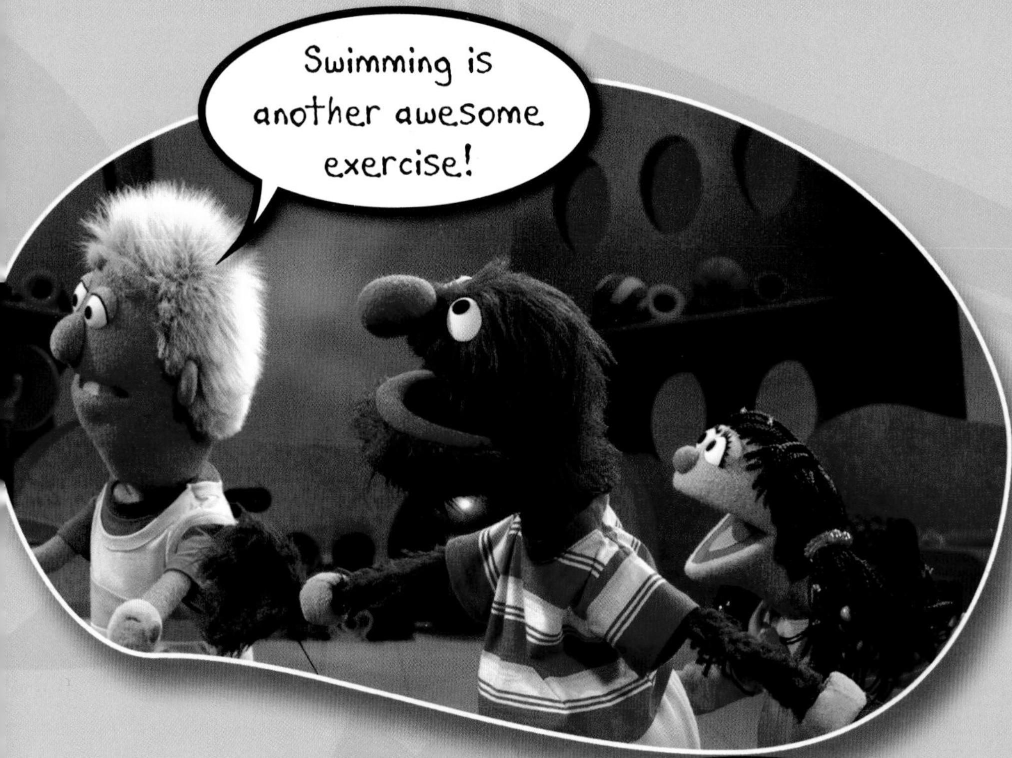
Swimming is another awesome exercise!

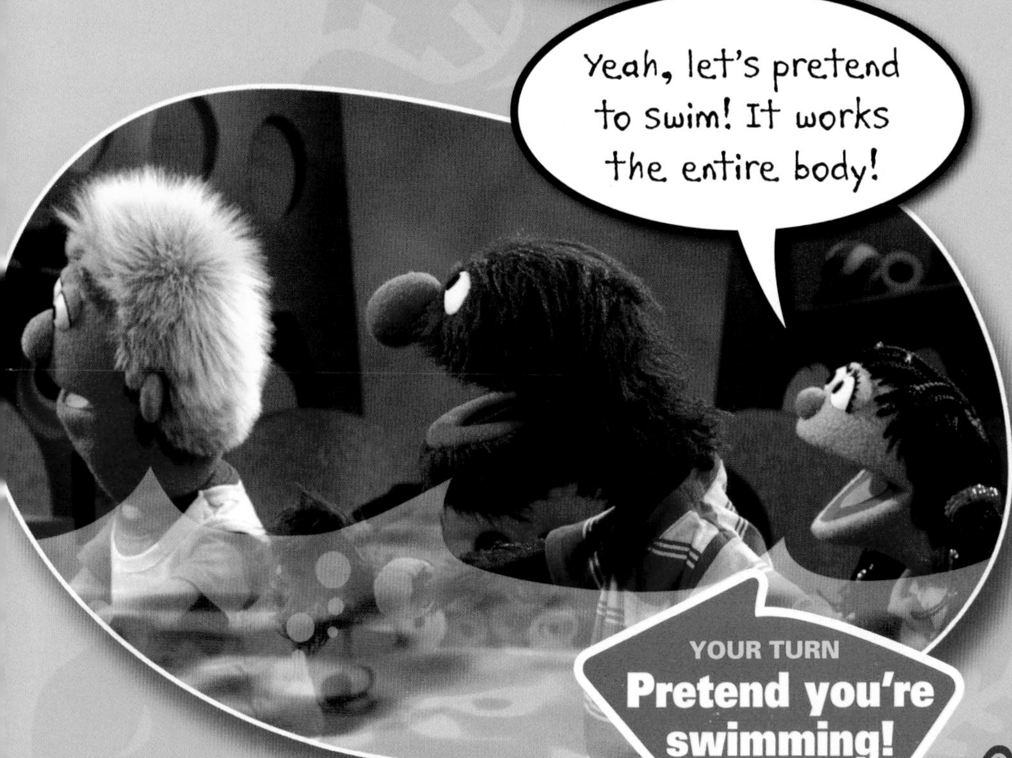
Yeah, let's pretend to swim! It works the entire body!

YOUR TURN

Pretend you're swimming!

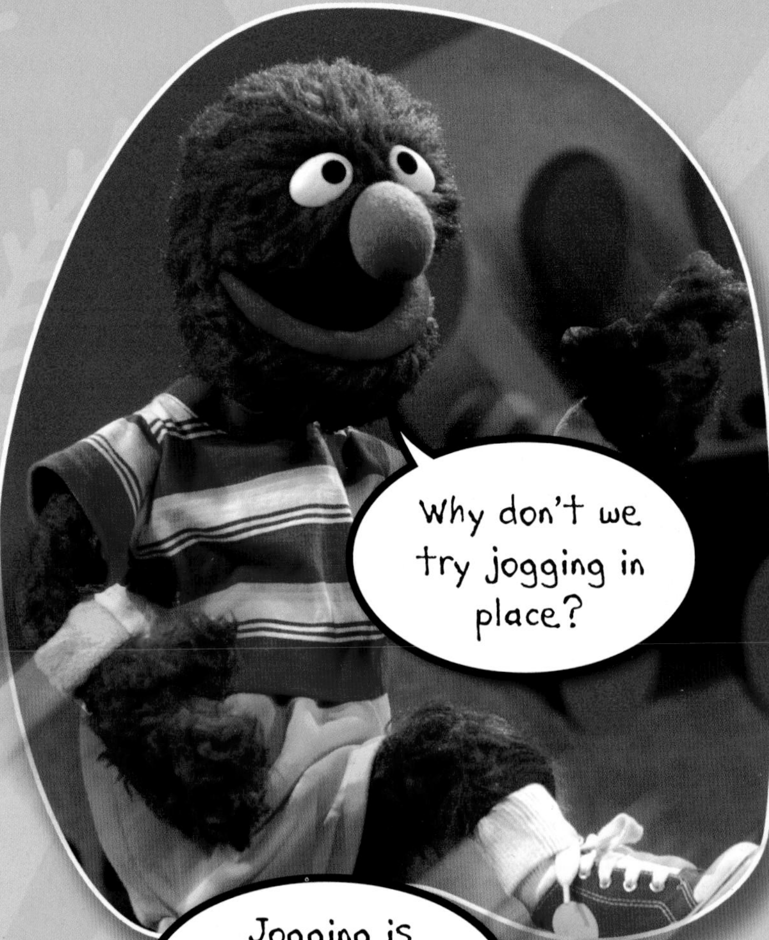
Why don't we try jogging in place?

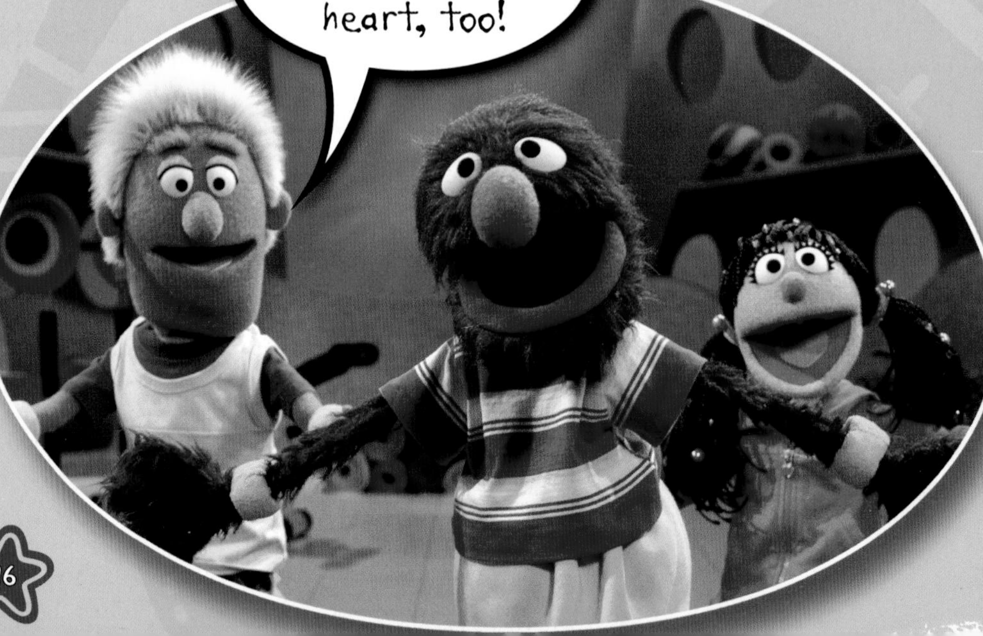
Jogging is good for your heart, too!

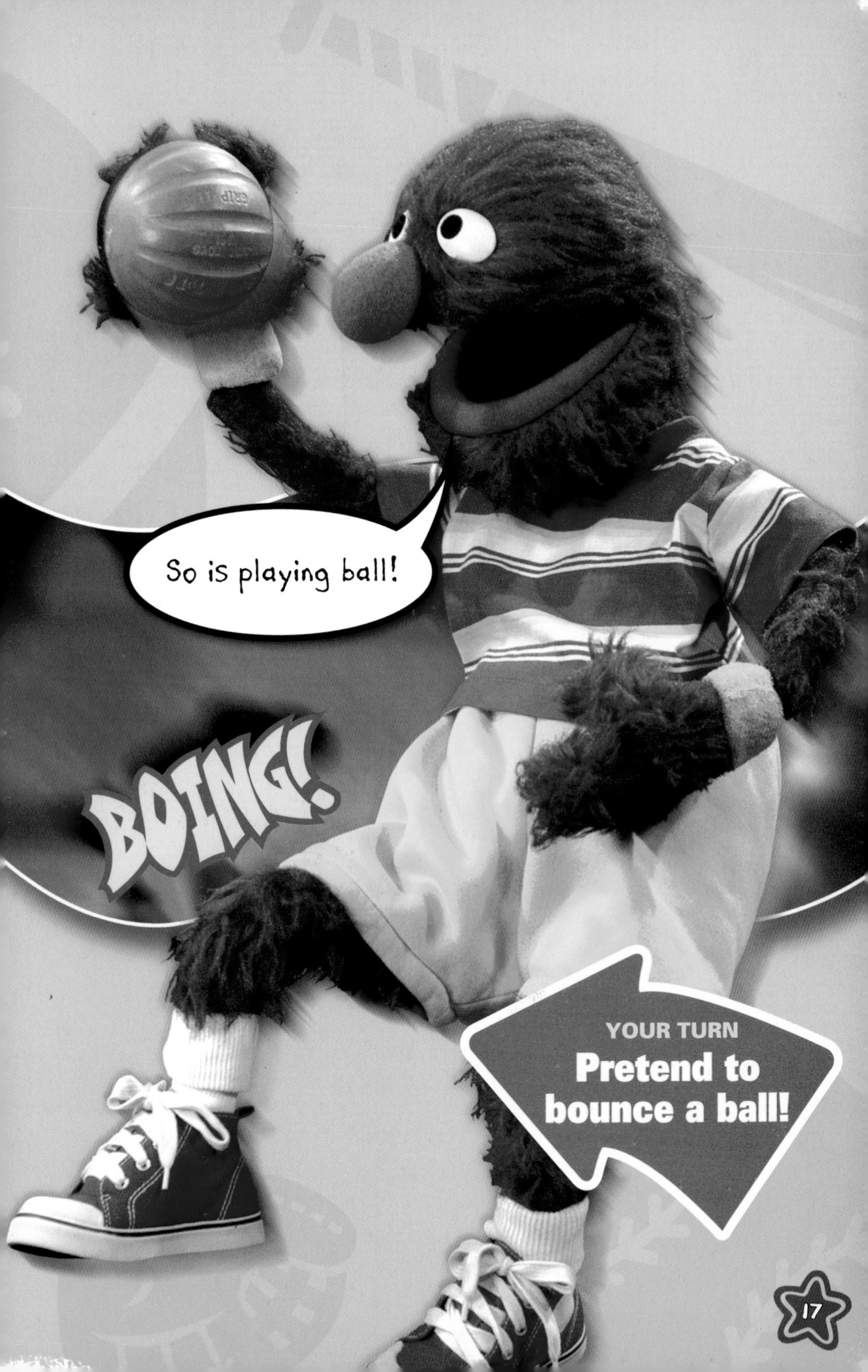
So is playing ball!
BOING!
YOUR TURN
Pretend to bounce a ball!

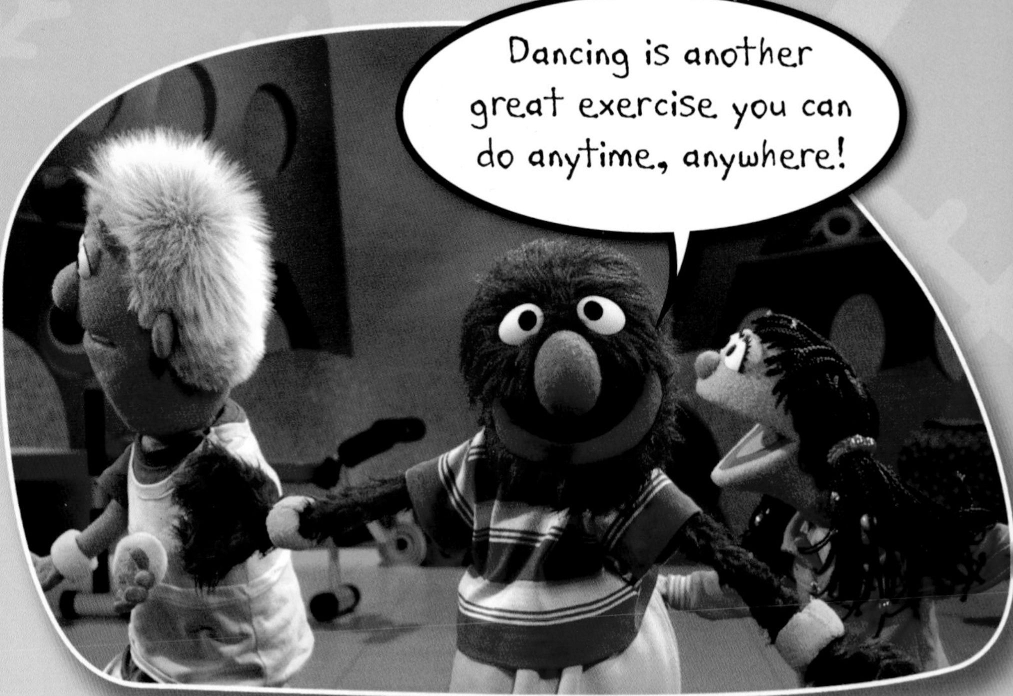
Dancing is another great exercise you can do anytime, anywhere!

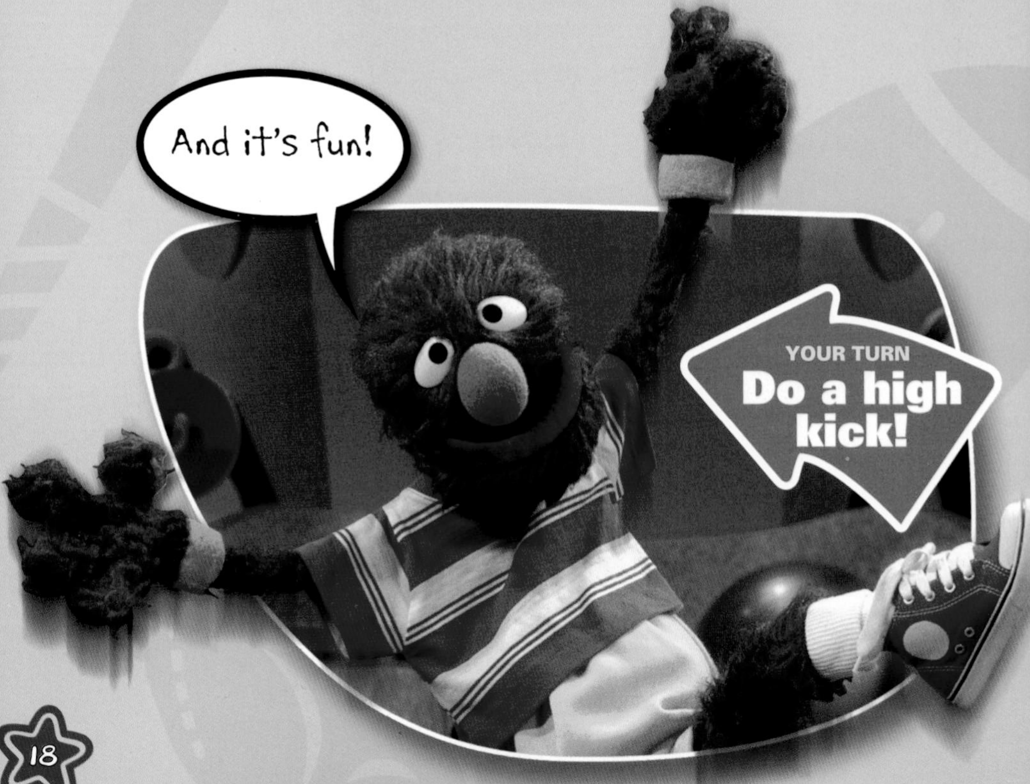
And it's fun!
YOUR TURN
Do a high kick!

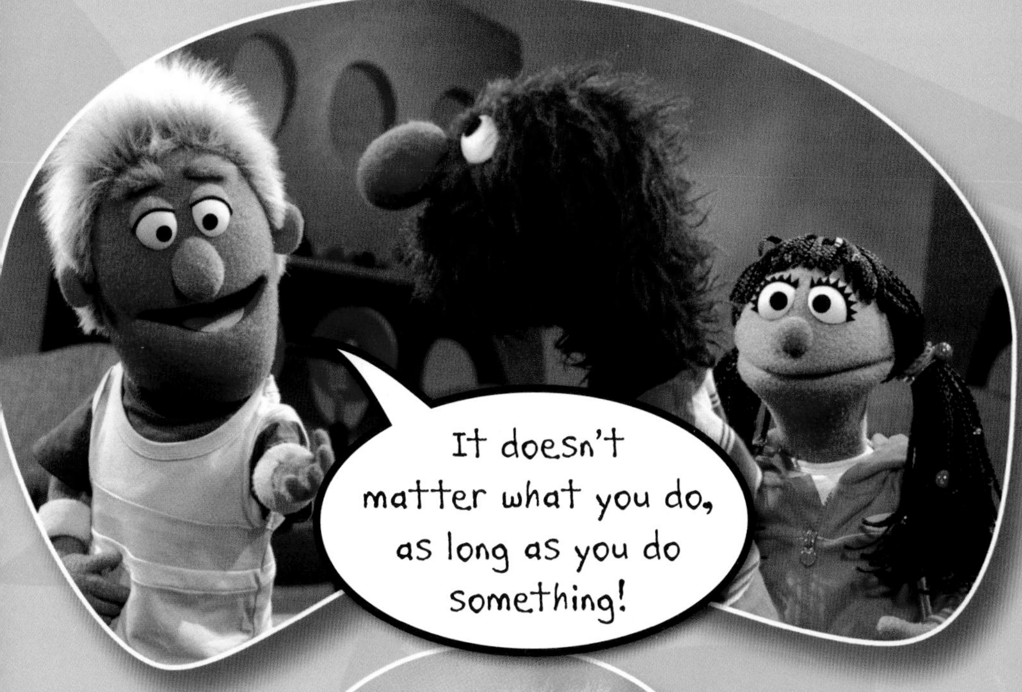
It doesn't matter what you do, as long as you do something!

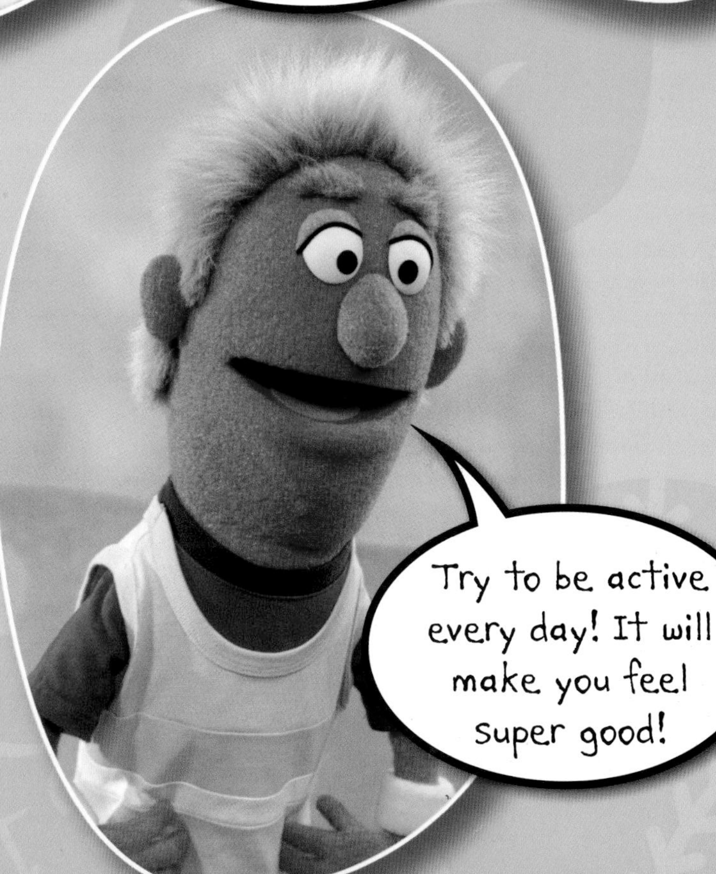
Try to be active every day! It will make you feel super good!

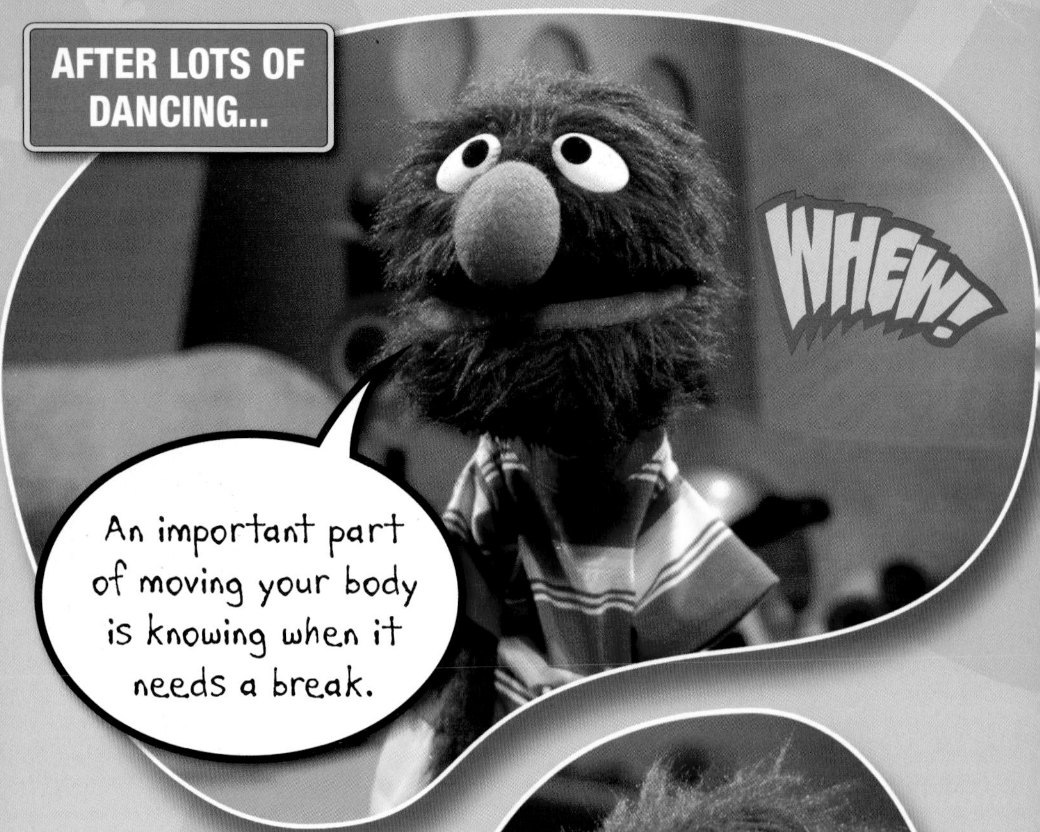
AFTER LOTS OF DANCING...
WHEW!
An important part of moving your body is knowing when it needs a break.

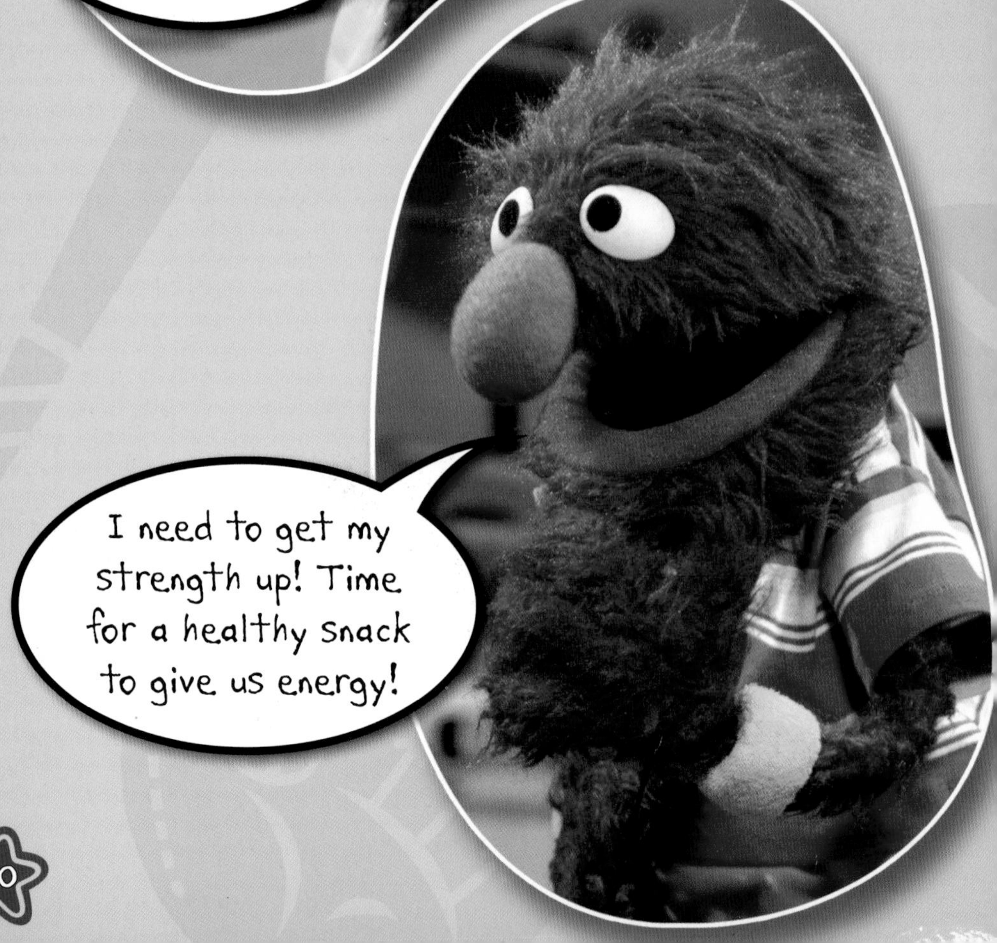
I need to get my strength up! Time for a healthy snack to give us energy!

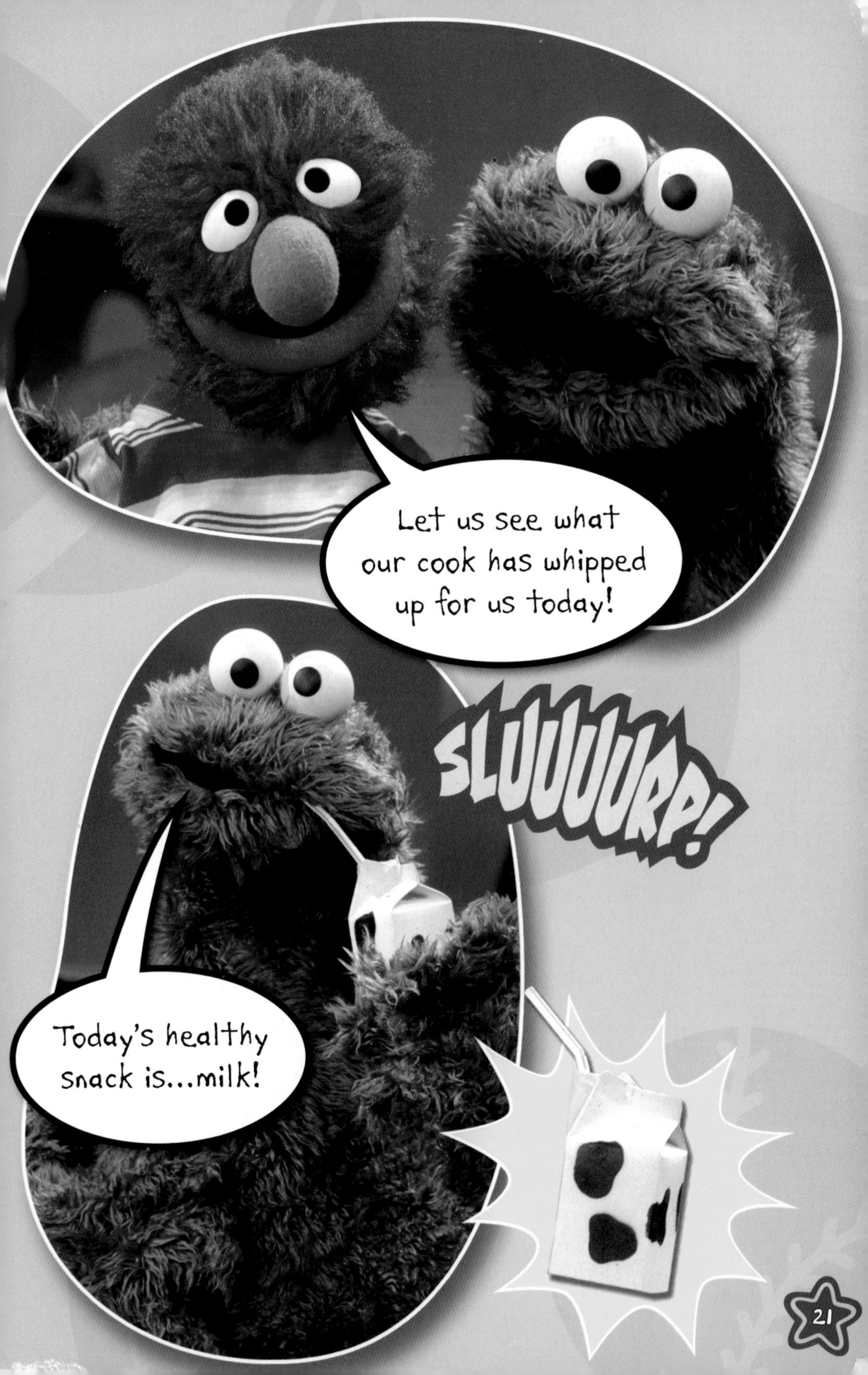
Let us see what our cook has whipped up for us today!
Today's healthy snack is...milk!
SLUUUURP!

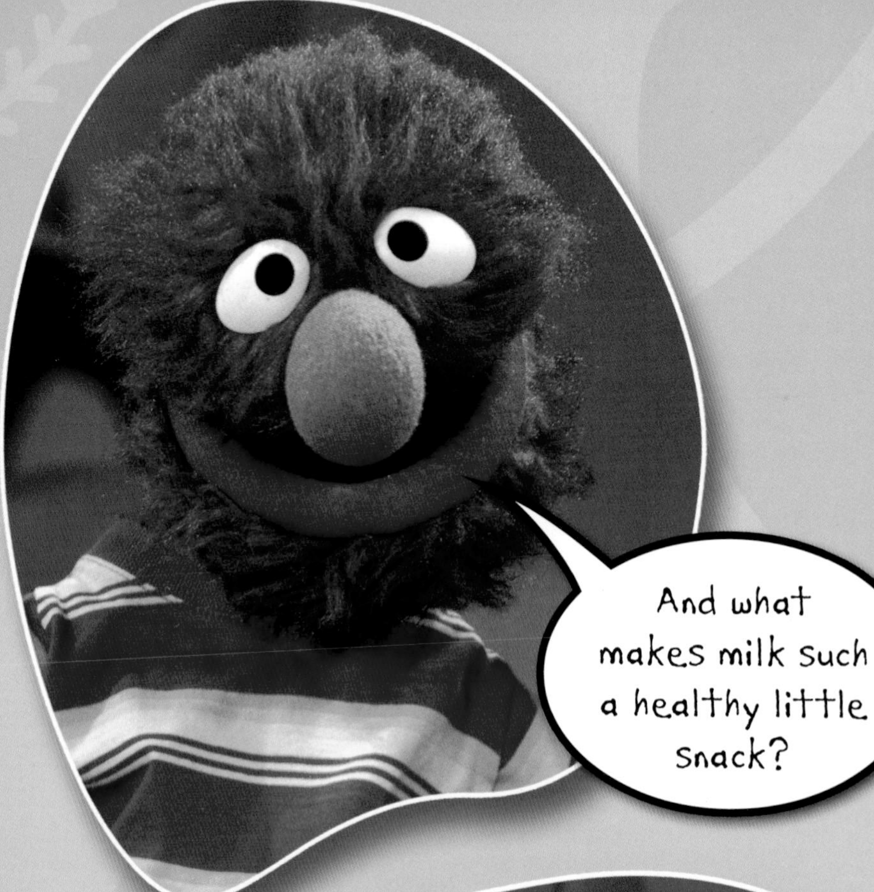
And what makes milk such a healthy little snack?

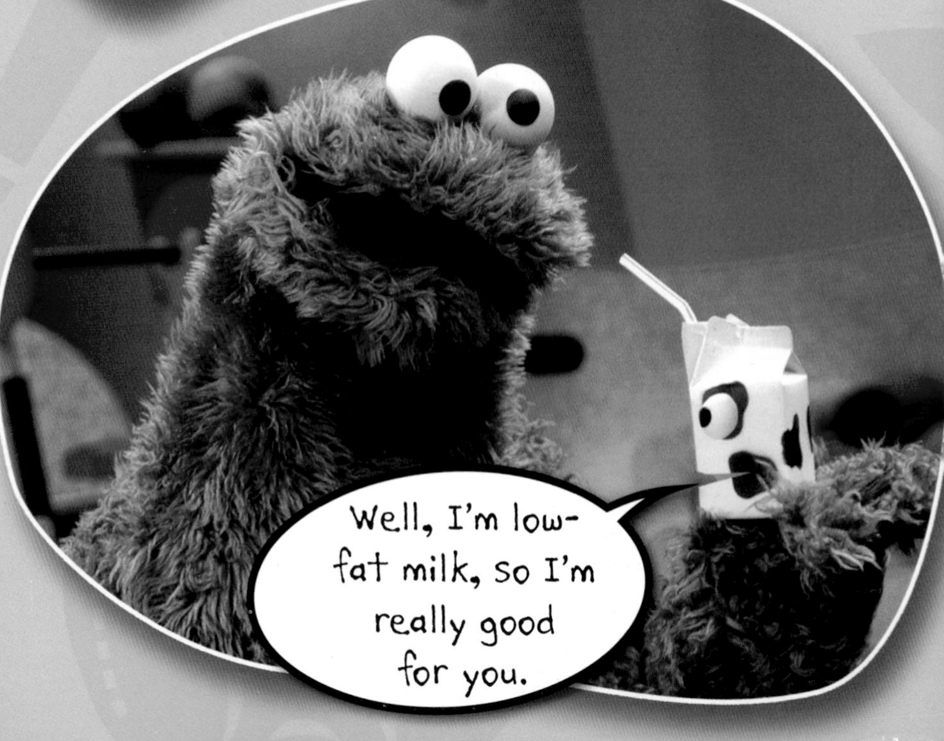
Well, I'm low-fat milk, so I'm really good for you.

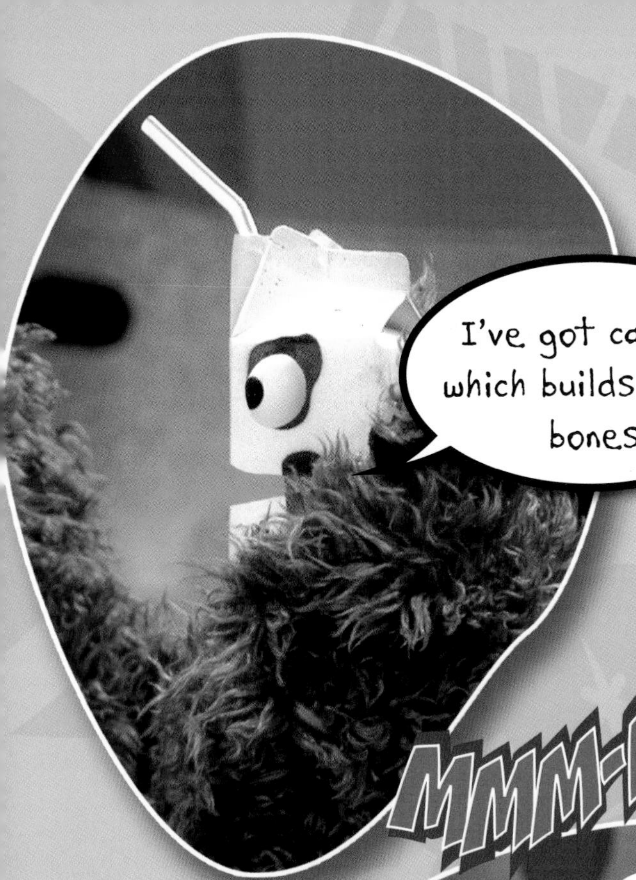
I've got calcium, which builds strong bones!
MMM-MMM!

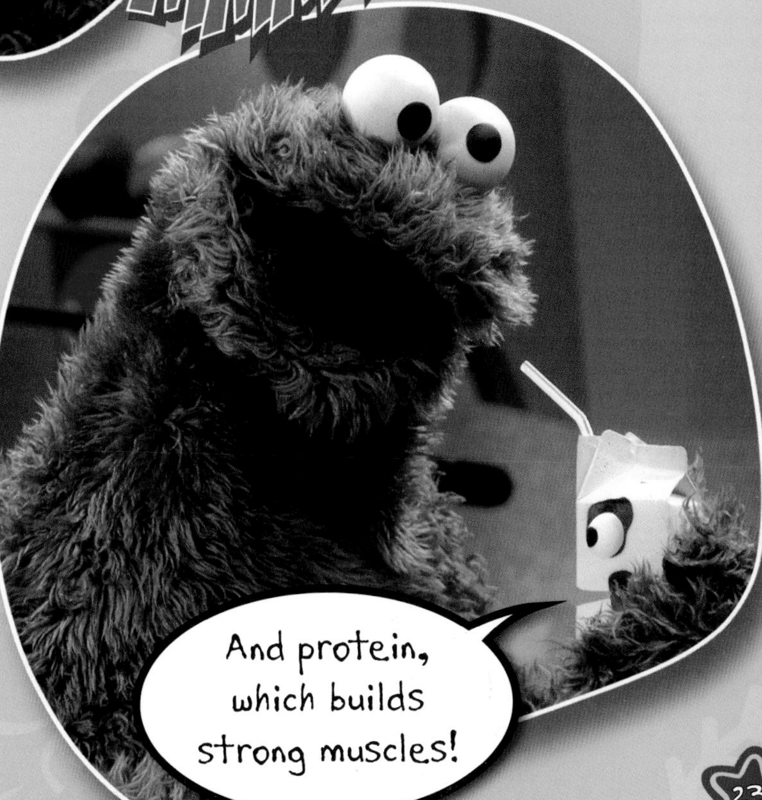
And protein, which builds strong muscles!

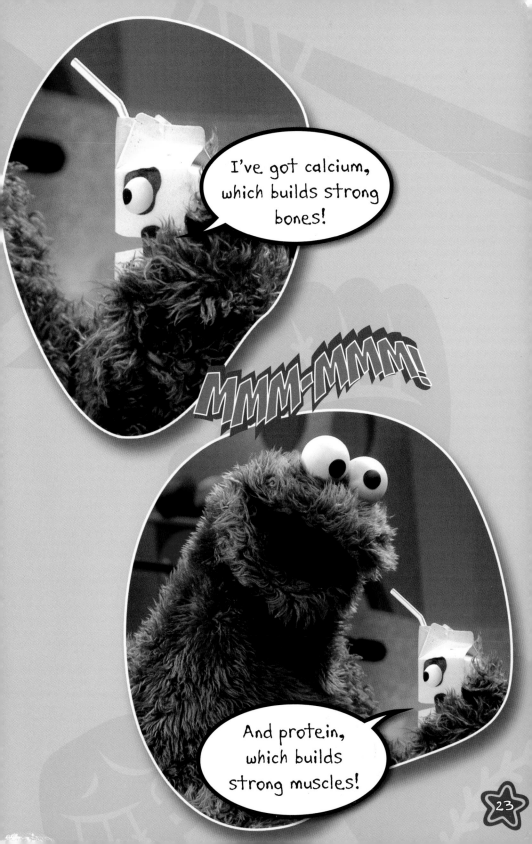

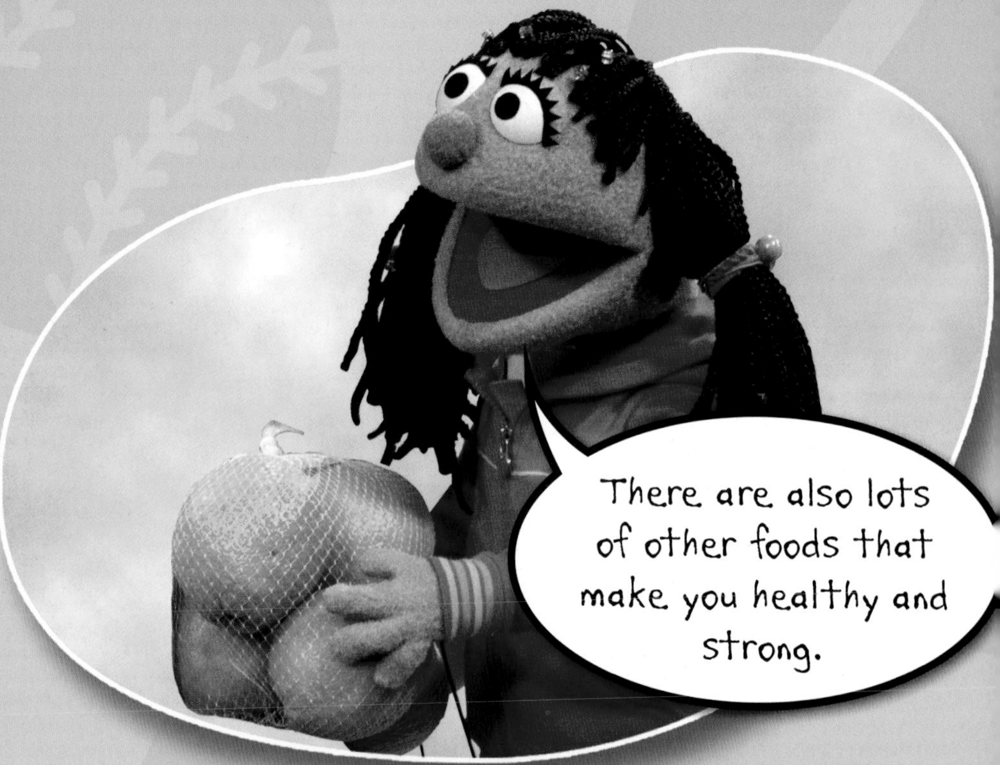
There are also lots of other foods that make you healthy and strong.

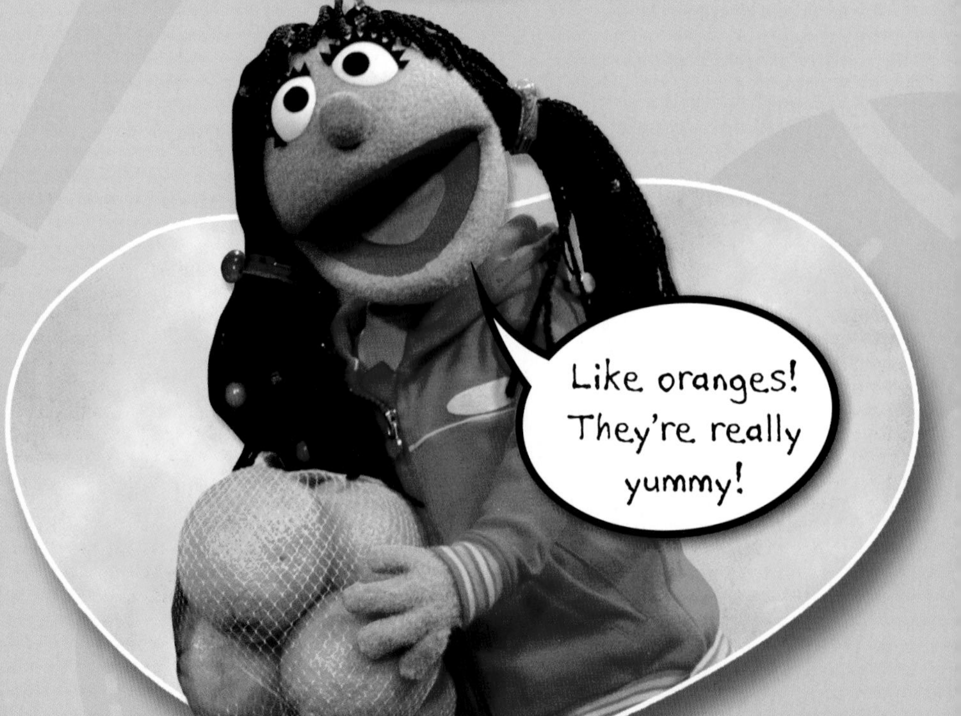
Like oranges! They're really yummy!

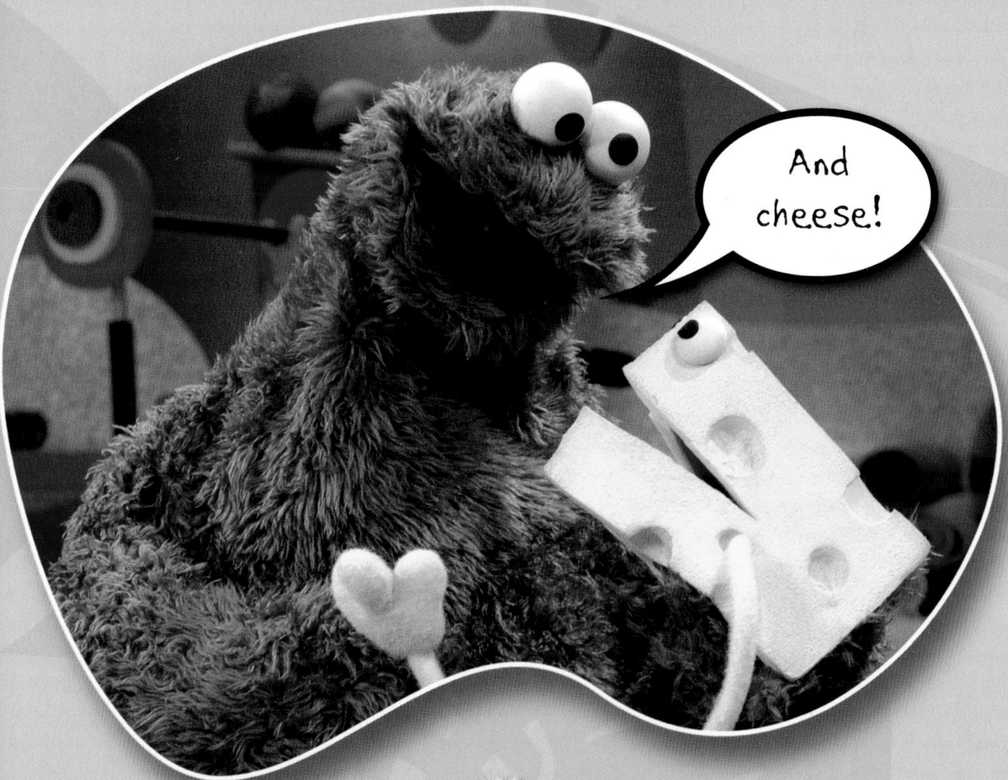
And cheese!

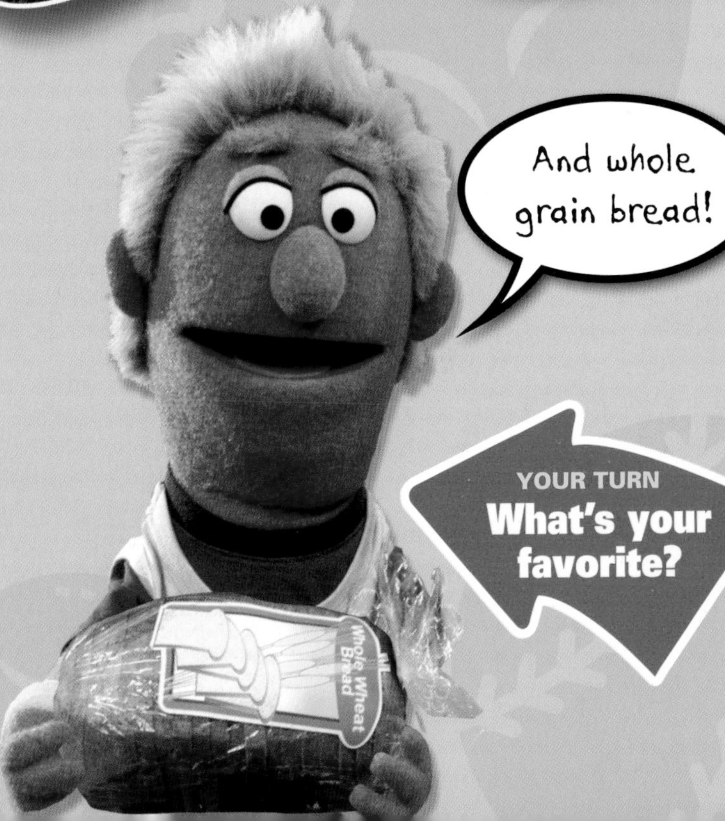
And whole grain bread!
Whole Wheat Bread

YOUR TURN
What's your favorite?

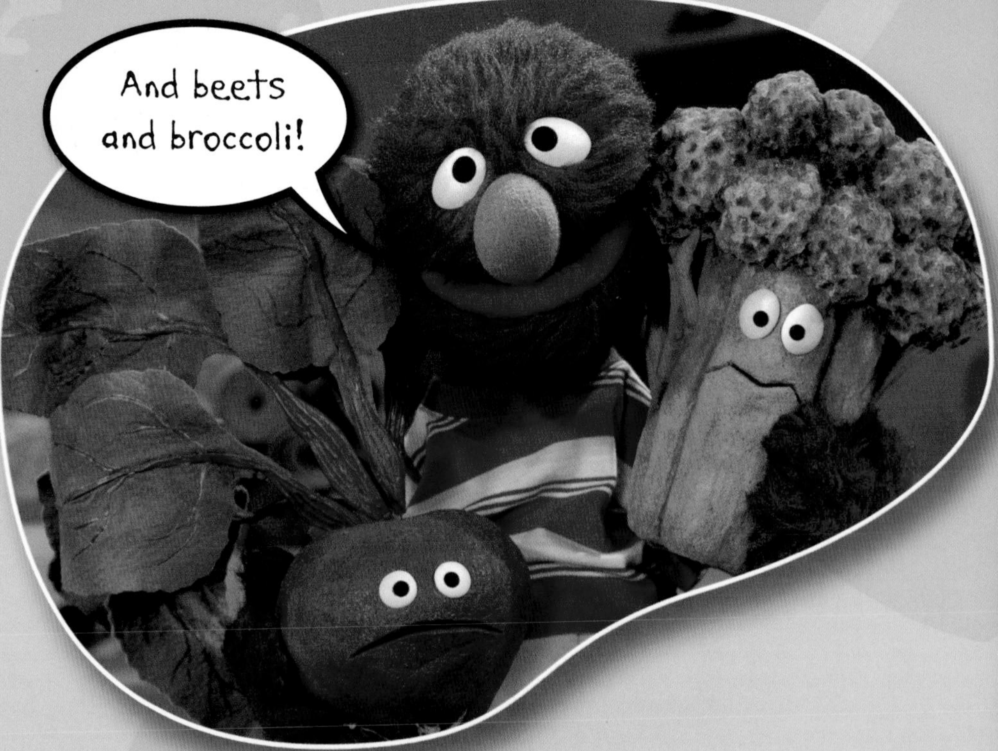
And beets and broccoli!

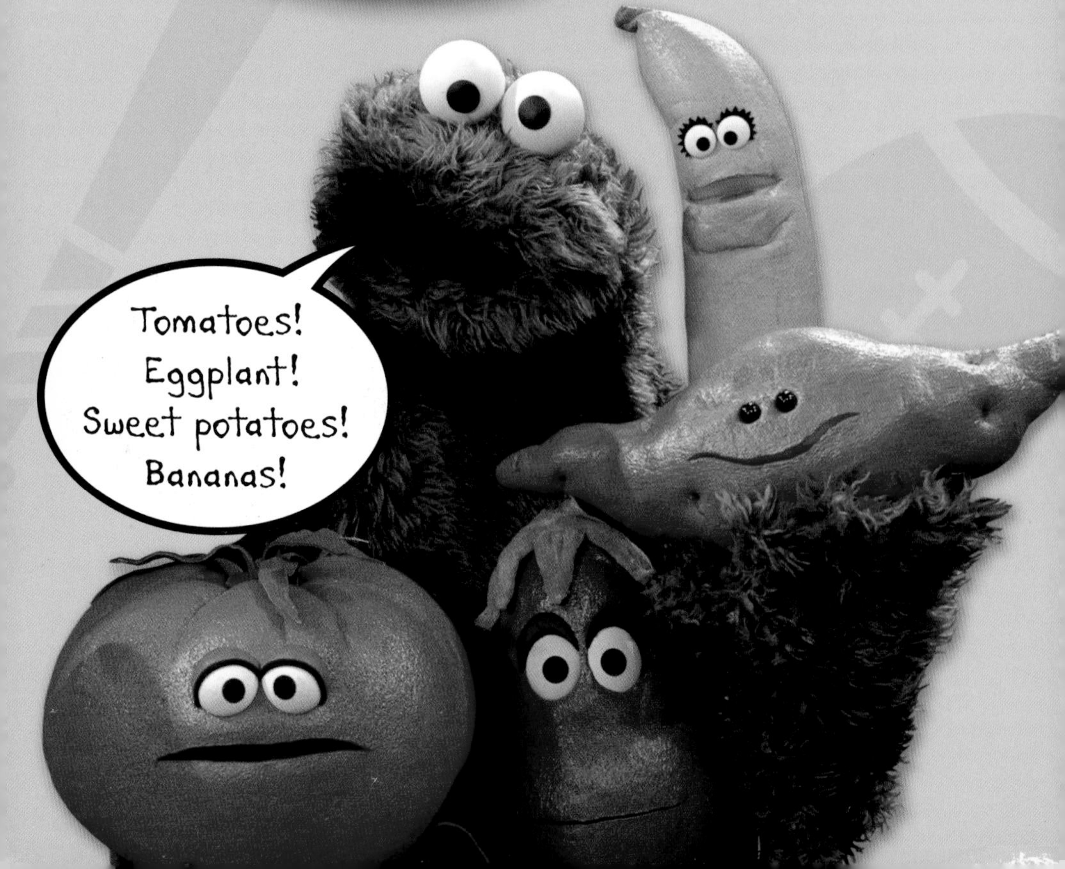
Tomatoes! Eggplant! Sweet potatoes! Bananas!

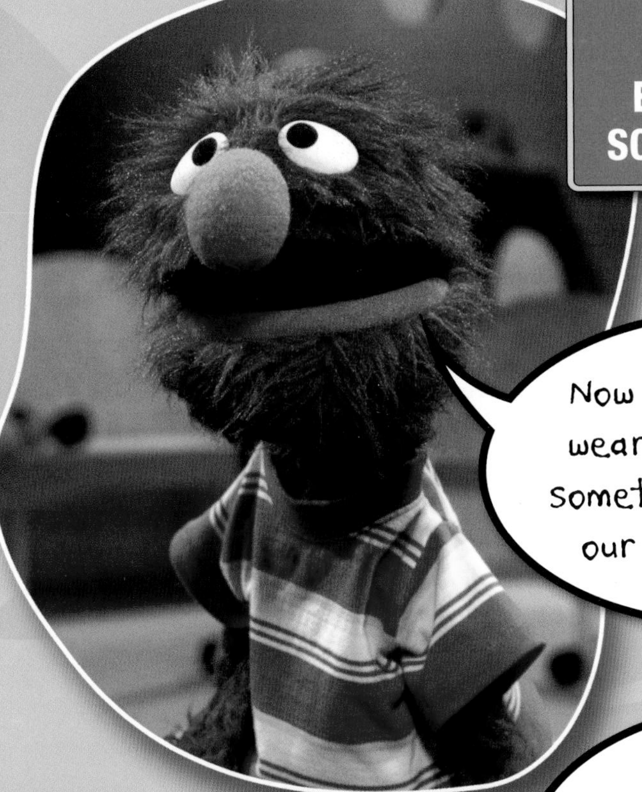
HEALTHY FOODS GIVE GROVER ENERGY TO JUMP SOME MORE. THEN...
Now let us rest our weary bodies and do something healthy for our minds instead.

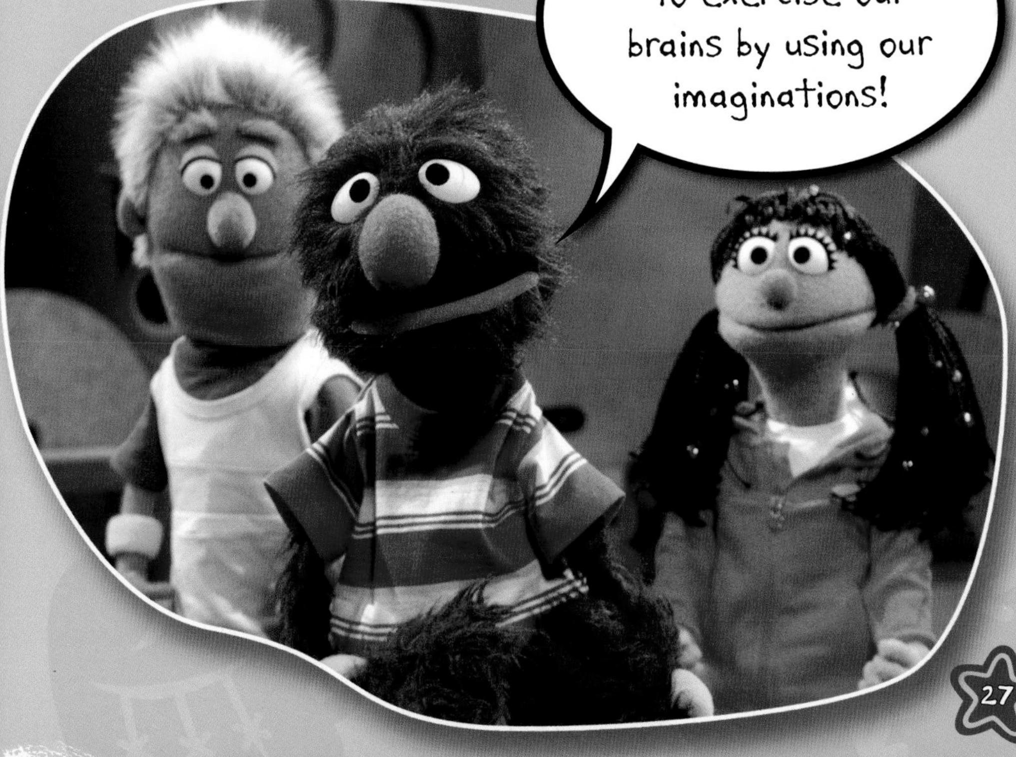
We are going to exercise our brains by using our imaginations!

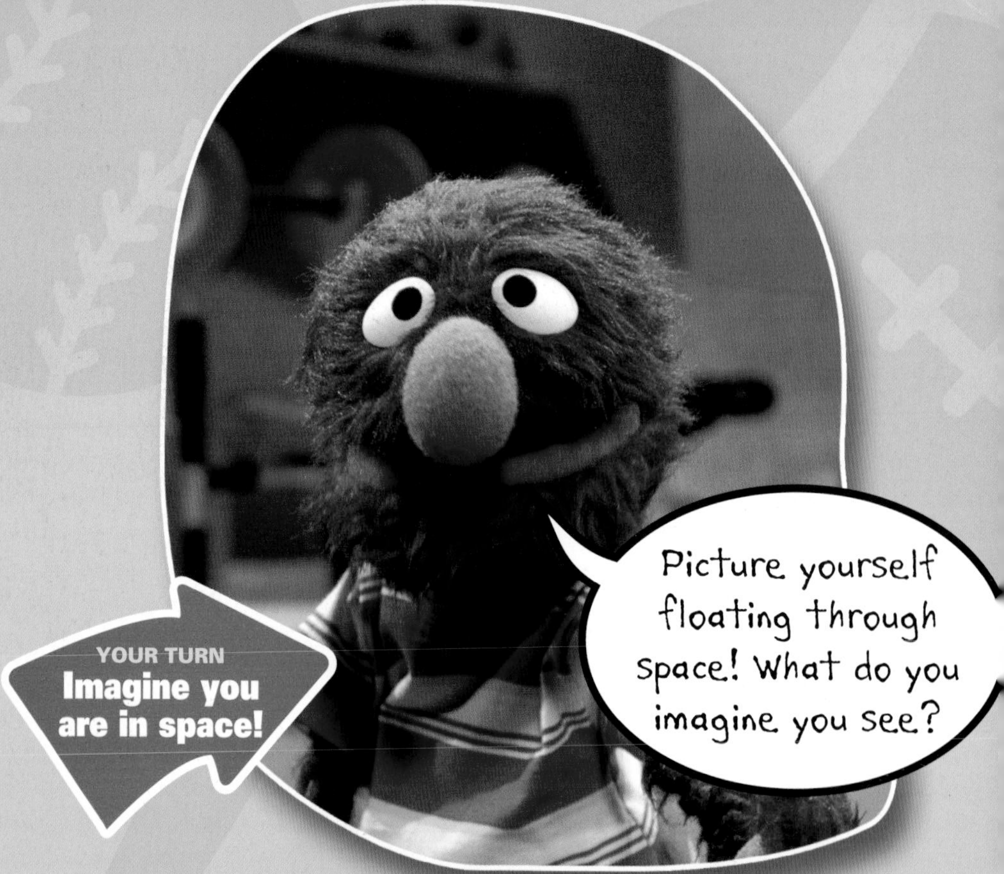
YOUR TURN
Imagine you are in space!
Picture yourself floating through space! What do you imagine you see?

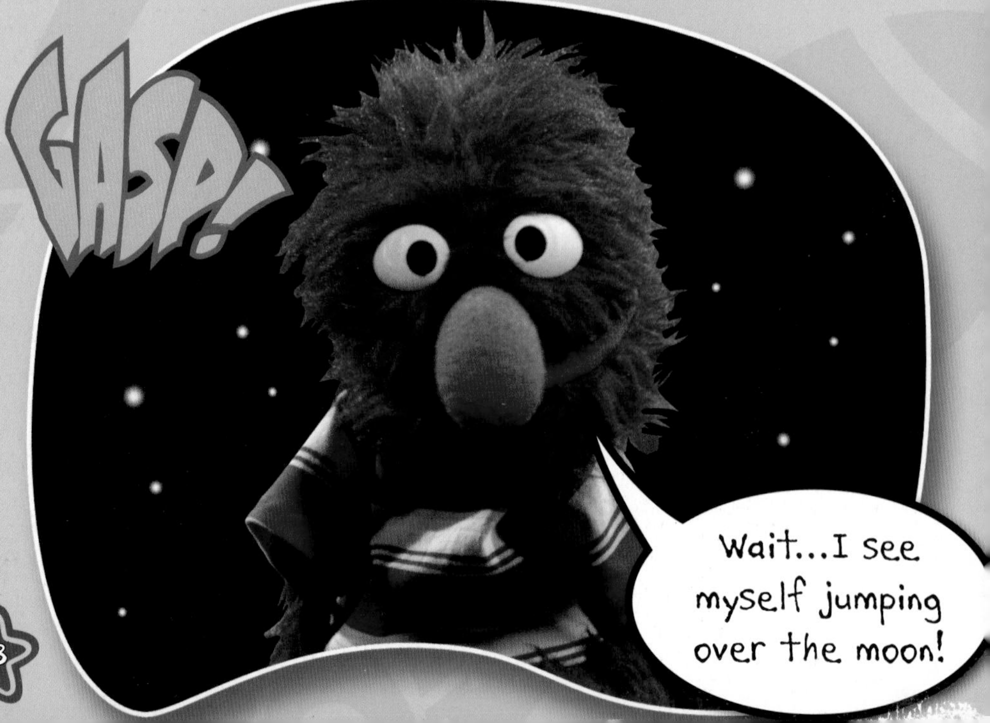
GASP!
Wait...I see myself jumping over the moon!

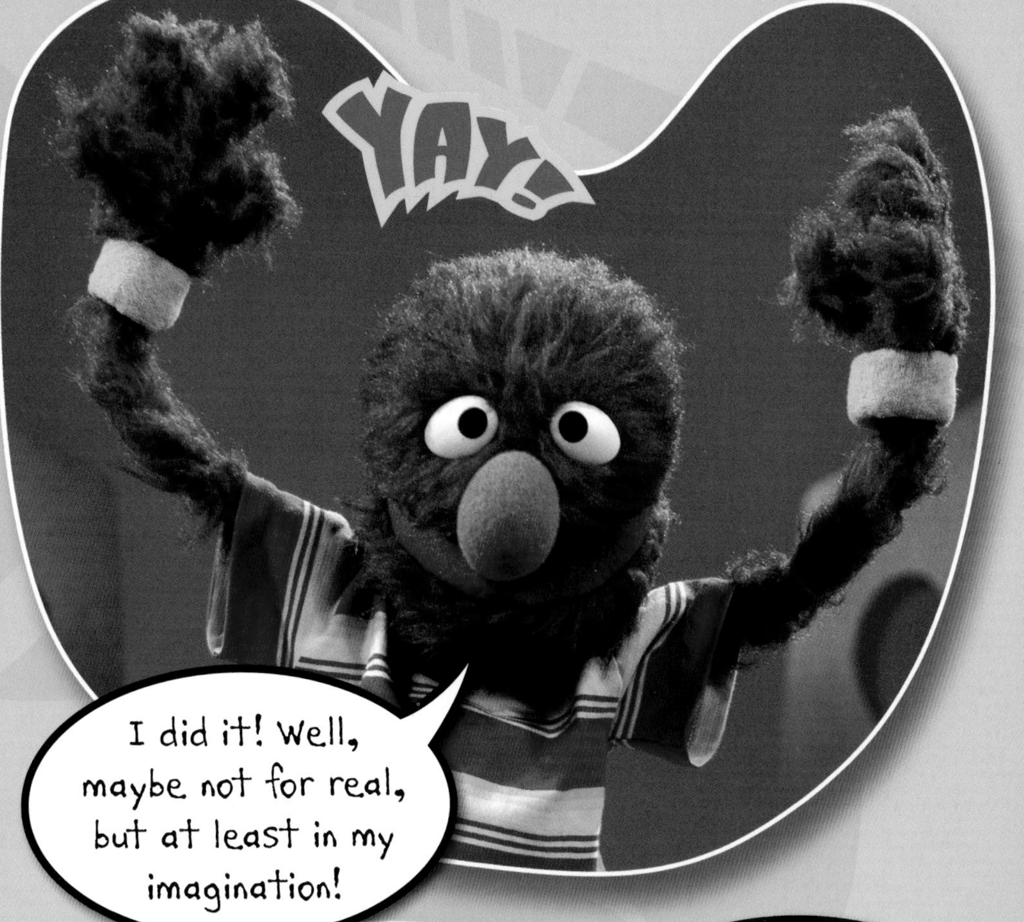
YAY!
I did it! Well, maybe not for real, but at least in my imagination!

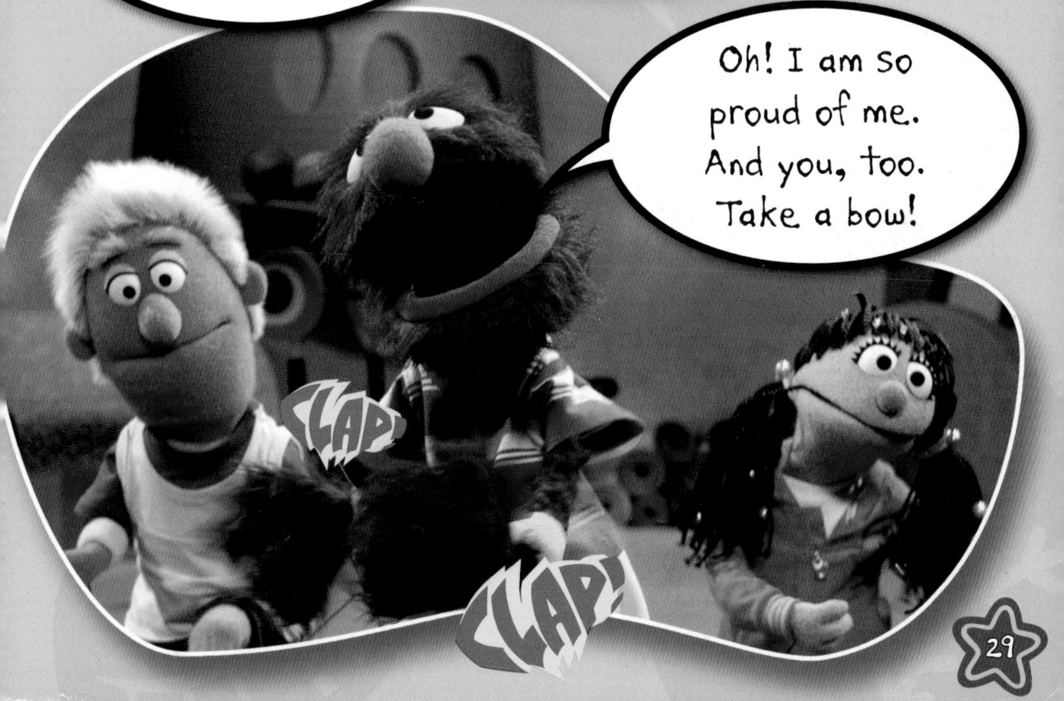
Oh! I am so proud of me. And you, too. Take a bow!
CLAP!
CLAP!

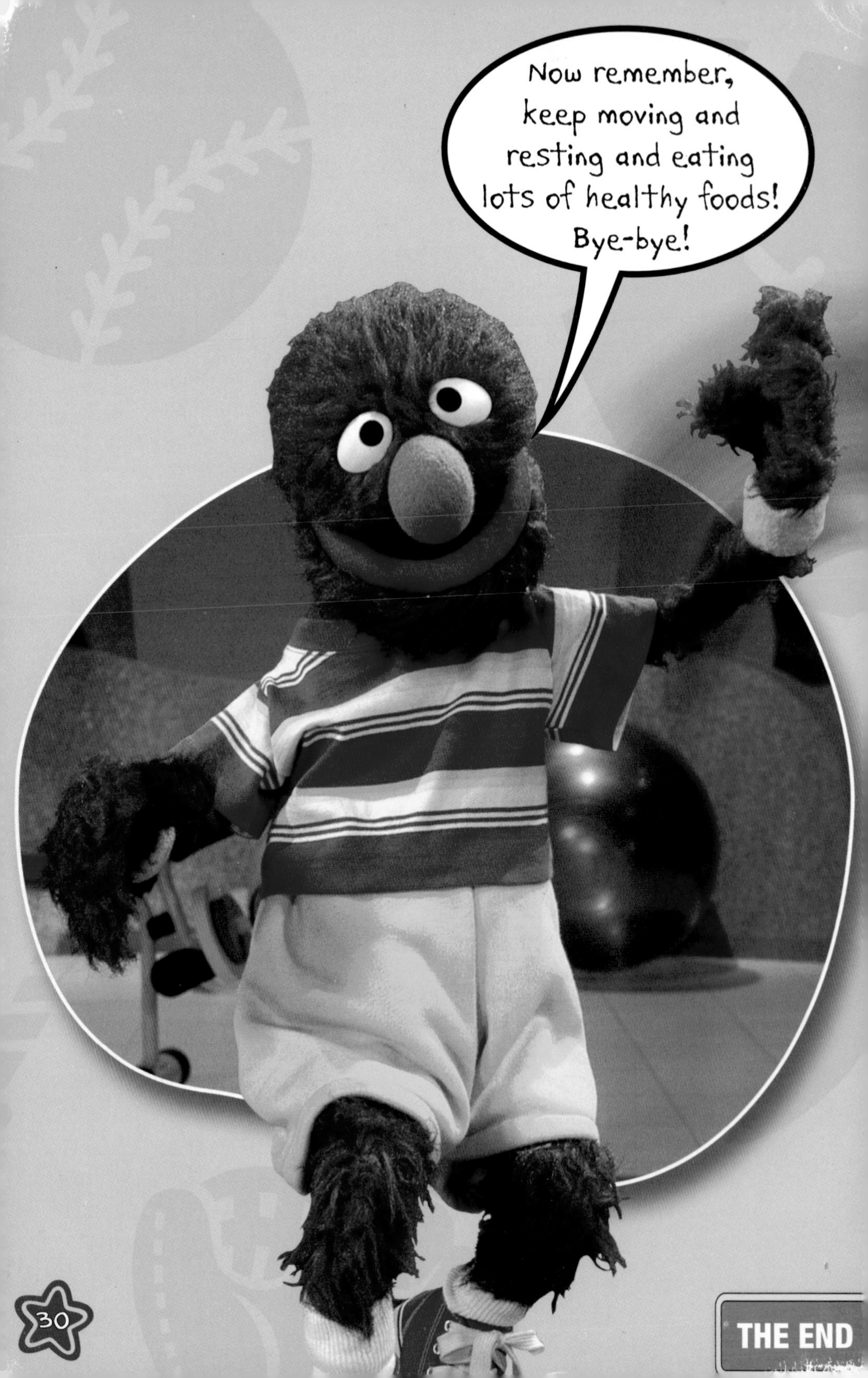
Now remember, keep moving and resting and eating lots of healthy foods! Bye-bye!
THE END